PENGUIN BOOKS

Story of the Eye

Georges Bataille, French essayist and novelist, was born in 1897. He was converted to Catholicism, then to Marxism and was interested in psychoanalysis and mysticism. As curator of the municipal library in Orléans, he led a relatively simple life, although he became involved, usually on the fringes, with the Surrealist movement. He founded the literary review *Critique* in 1946, which he edited until his death in 1962, and was also a founder of the review *Documents*, which published many of the leading Surrealist writers.

His writing is a mixture of poetry and philosophy, fantasy and history. It follows the mazes of an exceedingly rich and varied thought, of which the centre point is defined in *L'Expérience intérieure* (1943), part of *Summa A-theologica*. His first novel, *Story of the Eye*, was written under the pseudonym of Lord Auch. Bataille's other works include the novels *Blue of Noon* and *My Mother*, and the essays *Eroticism* and *Literature and Evil*.

Susan Sontag is one of America's best-known and most admired writers. Her books include the novels, *The Benefactor*, *Death Kit* and *The Volcano Lover*; a collection of stories, *I, etcetera*; a story, *The Way We Live Now*; and a play, *Alice in Bed*. Among her non-fiction books are collections of essays, *Against Interpretation*, *Styles of Radical Will*, *On Photography*, which won the National Book Critics' Circle Award, and *Under the Sign of Saturn*. She has also written and directed feature length films and staged plays in the United States and Europe.

Roland Barthes was born in 1915 and studied French literature and Classics at the University of Paris. After teaching French at universities in Romania and Egypt, he joined the Centre National de la Recherche Scientifique, where he devoted himself to research in sociology and lexicology. He later lectured at the École des Hautes Études on the sociology of signs, symbols and collective representations. Roland Barthes died in 1980. His publications include *On Racine*, *Writing Degree Zero*, *Elements of Semiology*, *Mythologies*, *S/Z*, *The Pleasure of Text* and *Sade/Fourier/Loyola*.

Georges Bataille

Story of the Eye
by Lord Auch

Translated by Joachim Neugroschal

With Essays by Susan Sontag and Roland Barthes

Penguin Books

PENGUIN BOOKS

Published by the Penguin Group
Penguin Books Ltd, 80 Strand, London WC2R 0RL, England
Penguin Putnam Inc., 375 Hudson Street, New York, New York 10014, USA
Penguin Books Australia Ltd, 250 Camberwell Road, Camberwell, Victoria 3124, Australia
Penguin Books Canada Ltd, 10 Alcorn Avenue, Toronto, Ontario, Canada M4V 3B2
Penguin Books India (P) Ltd, 11 Community Centre, Panchsheel Park, New Delhi – 110 017, India
Penguin Books (NZ) Ltd, Cnr Rosedale and Airborne Roads, Albany, Auckland, New Zealand
Penguin Books (South Africa) (Pty) Ltd, 24 Sturdee Avenue, Rosebank 2196, South Africa

Penguin Books Ltd, Registered Offices: 80 Strand, London WC2R 0RL, England

www.penguin.com

Story of the Eye first published in France as *Histoire de l'Oeil* 1928
The Pornographic Imagination first published by Martin Secker & Warburg Ltd
in *Styles of Radical Will* 1967
The Metaphor of the Eye first published in France as
Le Métaphore de l'Oeil in *Critique* 1963

First published in this edition by Marion Boyars Publishers Ltd 1979
Published in Penguin Books 1982
Reprinted in Penguin Classics 2001

10

Story of the Eye copyright © J.-J. Pauvert, 1967
This translation copyright © Urizen Books, 1977
The Pornographic Imagination copyright © Susan Sontag, 1967
The Metaphor of the Eye copyright © Roland Barthes, 1963
This translation copyright © Marion Boyars Publishers Ltd, 1979
All rights reserved

Printed in England by Clays Ltd, St Ives plc
Set in Monophoto Bembo

ISBN-13: 978-0-141-18538-5

Contents

STORY OF THE EYE

Publisher's Note

The shortness of this important erotic classic – now translated into English for the first time fifty years after its original French publication – enables us to include in this volume two essays that deal with the genre and style of *Story of the Eye:* Susan Sontag's essay on aspects of the literature of sex, *The Pornographic Imagination* (from 'Styles of Radical Will', 1967) explores a literary form that is, despite its manifold representation in English and Continental writing, seldom accepted in our puritan Anglo-American canon. Roland Barthes' *The Metaphor of the Eye* (from the magazine 'Critique', 1963) discusses in depth the language of *Story of the Eye,* a major example of French Surrealist writing, a movement which is at last beginning to receive serious critical attention in England and the United States.   M.B.

STORY OF THE EYE

Translator's Note

Story of the Eye was GEORGES BATAILLE'S first novel, and there were four editions, the first in 1928. The other three, known as the "new version", came out in 1940, 1941, and 1967. The "new version" differs so thoroughly in all details from the first edition that one can justifiably speak of two distinct books. Indeed, the Gallimard publication of the complete works includes both versions in its opening volume.

The English translation is based on the original version, but the "Outline for a Sequel" comes from the fourth edition.

Of all the editions, only the final, posthumous one bore the author's name. The other three were credited to Lord Auch, a pseudonym explained in Bataille's short prose piece *Le Petit* (1943). (The relevant part is included at the end of this section.)

J.N.

PART 1. THE TALE

1. The Cat's Eye

I grew up very much alone, and as far back as I recall I was frightened of anything sexual. I was nearly sixteen when I met Simone, a girl my own age, at the beach in X. Our families being distantly related, we quickly grew intimate. Three days after our first meeting, Simone and I were alone in her villa. She was wearing a black pinafore with a starched white collar. I began to realize that she shared my anxiety at seeing her, and I felt even more anxious that day because I hoped she would be stark naked under the pinafore.

She had black silk stockings on covering her knees, but I was unable to see as far up as the cunt (this name, which I always used with Simone, is, I think, by far the loveliest of the names for the vagina). It merely struck me that by slightly lifting the pinafore from behind, I might see her private parts unveiled.

Now in the corner of a hallway there was a saucer of milk for the cat. "Milk is for the pussy, isn't it?" said Simone. "Do you dare me to sit in the saucer?"

"I dare you," I answered, almost breathless.

The day was extremely hot. Simone put the saucer on a small bench, planted herself before me, and, with her eyes fixed on me, she sat down without my being able to see her burning buttocks under the skirt, dipping into the cool milk. The blood shot to my head, and I stood before her awhile, immobile and trembling, as she eyed my stiff cock bulging in my trousers. Then I lay down at her feet without her stirring, and for the first time, I saw her "pink and dark" flesh cooling in the white milk. We remained motionless, both of us equally overwhelmed....

Suddenly, she got up, and I saw the milk dripping down her thighs to the stockings. She wiped herself evenly with a handkerchief as she stood over my head with one foot on the small bench, and I vigorously rubbed my cock through the trousers while writhing amorously on the floor. We reached orgasm at almost the same instant without even touching one another. But when her mother came home, I was sitting in a low armchair, and I took advantage of the moment when the girl tenderly snuggled in her mother's arms: I lifted the back of her pinafore, unseen, and thrust my hand under her cunt between her two burning legs.

I dashed home, eager to masturbate again. The next day there were such dark rings around my eyes that Simone, after peering at me for a while, buried her head in my shoulder and said earnestly: "I don't want you to toss off any more without me."

Thus a love life started between the girl and myself, and it was so intimate and so intense that we could hardly let a week go by without meeting. And yet we virtually never talked about it. I realized that her feelings at seeing me were the same as mine at seeing her, but I found it difficult to have things out. I remember that one day, when we were in a car tooling along at top speed, we crashed into a cyclist, an apparently very young and very pretty girl. Her head was almost totally ripped off by the wheels. For a long time, we were parked a few yards beyond without getting out, fully absorbed in the sight of the corpse. The horror and despair at so much bloody flesh, nauseating in part, and in part very beautiful, was fairly equivalent to our usual impression upon seeing one another. Simone was tall and lovely. She was usually very natural; there was nothing heartbreaking in her eyes or her voice. But on a sensual level, she so bluntly craved any upheaval that the faintest call from the senses gave her a look directly suggestive of all things linked to deep sexuality, such as blood, suffocation, sudden terror, crime; things indefinitely destroying human bliss and honesty. I first saw her mute and absolute spasm (which I shared) the day she sat down in the saucer of milk. True, we only exchanged fixed stares at analogous moments. But we never calmed down or played except in the brief relaxed minutes after an orgasm.

I ought to say, nevertheless, that we waited a long time before copulating. We merely took any opportunity to indulge in unusual acts. We did not lack modesty—on the contrary—but something urgently drove us to defy modesty together as immodestly as possible. Thus, no sooner had she asked me never to toss off again by myself (we had met on top of a cliff), than she pulled down my pants and had me stretch out on the ground. She tucked her dress up, mounted my belly with her back towards my face, and let herself go, while I thrust my finger, lubricated with my young sperm, into her cunt. Next, she lay down, with her head under my cock between my legs, and thrusting her cunt in the air, she brought her body down towards me, while I raised my head to the level of that cunt: her knees found support on my shoulders.

"Can't you pee up to my cunt?" she said.

"Yes," I answered, "but with you like this, it'll get on your dress and your face."

"So what," she concluded. And I did as she said, but no sooner was I done than I flooded her again, this time with fine white come.

Meanwhile, the smell of the sea mixed with the smell of wet linen, our naked bodies, and the come. Evening was gathering, and we stayed in that extraordinary position, tranquil and motionless, when all at once we heard steps crushing the grass.

"Please don't move, please," Simone begged.

The steps halted, but it was impossible to see who was approaching. Our breathing had stopped together. Simone's arse, raised aloft, did strike me as an all-powerful entreaty, perfect as it was, with its two narrow, delicate buttocks and its deep crevice; and I never doubted for an instant that the unknown man or woman would soon give in and feel compelled to masturbate endlessly while watching that behind. Now the steps resumed, faster this time, almost running, and suddenly a ravishing blond girl loomed into view: Marcelle, the purest and most affecting of our friends. But we were too strongly contracted in our dreadful positions to move even a hair's breadth, and it was our unhappy friend who suddenly collapsed and huddled in the grass amid sobs. Only now did we tear loose from our extravagant embrace to hurl ourselves upon a self-abandoned body. Simone hiked up the skirt, ripped off the panties, and drunkenly showed me a new cunt, as lovely and pure as her own: I kissed it furiously while finger fucking Simone, whose legs closed around the hips of that strange Marcelle, who no longer hid anything but her sobs.

"Marcelle," I exclaimed, "please, please don't cry. I want you to kiss me on the mouth...."

Simone, for her part, stroked the girl's lovely smooth hair, covering her body with fond kisses.

Meanwhile the sky had turned quite thundery, and, with nightfall, huge raindrops began plopping down, bringing relief from the harshness of a torrid, airless day. The sea was loudly raging, outroared by long rumbles of thunder, while flashes of lightning, bright as day, kept brusquely revealing the two pleasured cunts of the now silent girls. A brutal frenzy drove our three bodies. Two young mouths fought over my arse, my balls, and my cock, but I still kept pushing apart female legs wet with saliva and come, splaying them as if writhing out of a monster's grip, and yet that monster was nothing but the utter violence of my movements. The hot rain was finally pouring down and streaming over our fully exposed bodies. Huge booms of thunder shook us, heightening our fury, wresting forth our cries of rage, which each flash accompanied with a glimpse of our sexual parts. Simone had found a mud puddle, and was smearing herself wildly: she was jerking off with the earth and coming violently, whipped by the downpour, my head locked in her soil-covered legs, her face wallowing in the puddle, where she was brutally churning Marcelle's cunt, one arm around Marcelle's hips, the hand yanking the thigh, forcing it open.

2. The Antique Wardrobe

That was the period when Simone developed a mania for breaking eggs with her behind. She would do a headstand on an armchair in the parlour, her back against the chair's back, her legs bent towards me, while I jerked off in order to come in her face. I would put the egg right on the hole in her arse, and she would skillfully amuse herself by shaking it in the deep crack of her buttocks. The moment my come shot out and trickled down her eyes, her buttocks would squeeze together and she would come while I smeared my face abundantly in her ass.

Very soon, of course, her mother, who might enter the villa parlour at any moment, did catch us in our unusual act. But still, the first time this fine woman stumbled upon us, she was content, despite having led an exemplary life, to gape wordlessly, so that we

Waterstone's

Exchange and refund policy

Waterstone's is happy to exchange or refund your items on presentation of a valid receipt. Goods must be returned within 21 days of purchase.

Shop online at Waterstones.com
Free UK delivery to store

Waterstone's

Exchange and refund policy

Waterstone's is happy to exchange or refund your items on presentation of a valid receipt. Goods must be returned within 21 days of purchase.

Shop online at Waterstones.com
Free UK delivery to store

Waterstone's

Exchange and refund policy

did not notice a thing. I suppose she was too flabbergasted to speak. But when we were done and trying to clean up the mess, we noticed her standing in the doorway.

"Pretend there's no one there," Simone told me, and she went on wiping her behind.

And indeed, we blithely strolled out as though the woman had been reduced to a family portrait.

A few days later, however, when Simone was doing gymnastics with me in the rafters of a garage, she pissed on her mother, who had the misfortune to stop underneath without seeing her. The sad widow got out of the way and gazed at us with such dismal eyes and such a desperate expression that she egged us on, that is to say, simply, with Simone bursting into laughter, crouching on all fours on the beams and exposing her cunt to my face, I uncovered that cunt completely and masturbated while looking at it.

More than a week had passed without our seeing Marcelle, when we ran into her on the street one day. The blonde girl, timid and naively pious, blushed so deeply at seeing us, that Simone embraced her with uncommon tenderness.

"Please forgive me, Marcelle," she murmured. "What happened the other day was absurd, but that doesn't mean we can't be friends now. I promise we'll never lay a hand on you again."

Marcelle, who had an unusual lack of will power, agreed to join us for tea with some other friends at our place. But instead of tea, we drank quantities of chilled champagne.

The sight of Marcelle blushing had completely overwhelmed us. We understood one another, Simone and I, and we were certain that from now on nothing would make us shrink from achieving our ends. Besides Marcelle, there were three other pretty girls and two boys here. The oldest of the eight being not quite seventeen, the beverage soon took effect; but aside from Simone and myself, they were not as excited as we wanted them to be. A gramophone rescued us from our predicament. Simone, dancing a frenzied Charleston by herself, showed everyone her legs up to her cunt, and when the other girls were asked to dance a solo in the same way, they were in too good a mood to require coaxing. They did have panties on, but the panties bound the cunt laxly without hiding much. Only Marcelle, intoxicated and silent, refused to dance.

Finally, Simone, pretending to be dead drunk, crumpled a tablecloth and, lifting it up, she offered to make a bet.

"I bet," she said, "that I can pee into the tablecloth in front of everyone."

It was basically a ridiculous party of mostly turbulent and boastful youngsters. One of the boys challenged her, and it was agreed that the winner would fix the penalty.... Naturally, Simone did not waver for an instant, she richly soaked the tablecloth. But this stunning act visibly rattled her to the quick, so that all the young fools started gasping.

"Since the winner decides the penalty," said Simone to the loser, "I am now going to pull down your trousers in front of everyone."

Which happened without a hitch. When his trousers were off, his shirt was likewise removed (to keep him from looking ridiculous). All the same, nothing serious had occurred as yet: Simone had scarcely run a light hand over her young friend, who was dazzled, drunk, and naked. Yet all she could think of was Marcelle, who for several moments now had been begging me to let her leave.

"We promised we wouldn't touch you, Marcelle. Why do you want to leave?"

"Just because," she replied stubbornly, a violent rage gradually overcoming her.

All at once, to everyone's horror, Simone fell upon the floor. A convulsion shook her harder and harder, her clothes were in disarray, her bottom stuck in the air, as though she were having an epileptic fit. But rolling about at the foot of the boy she had undressed, she mumbled almost inarticulately:

"Piss on me.... Piss on my cunt...." she repeated, with a kind of thirst.

Marcelle gaped at this spectacle: she blushed again, her face was blood-red. But then she said to me, without even looking at me, that she wanted to take off her dress. I half tore it off, and straight after, her underwear. All she had left was her stockings and belt, and after I fingered her cunt a bit and kissed her on the mouth, she glided across the room to a large antique bridal wardrobe, where she shut herself in after whispering a few words to Simone.

She wanted to toss off in the wardrobe and was pleading to be left in peace.

I ought to say that we were all very drunk and completely bowled over by what had been going on. The naked boy was being sucked by a girl. Simone, standing with her dress tucked up, was rubbing her bare cunt against the wardrobe, in which a girl was audibly masturbating with brutal gasps. And all at once, something incredible happened, a strange swish of water, followed by a trickle and a stream from under the wardrobe door: poor Marcelle was pissing in her wardrobe while masturbating. But the explosion of totally drunken guffaws that ensued rapidly degenerated into a debauche of tumbling bodies, lofty legs and arses, wet skirts and come. Guffaws emerged like foolish and involuntary hiccups but scarcely managed to interrupt a brutal onslaught on cunts and cocks. And yet soon we could hear Marcelle dismally sobbing alone, louder and louder, in the make-shift pissoir that was now her prison.

Half an hour later, when I was less drunk, it dawned on me that I ought to let Marcelle out of her wardrobe: the unhappy girl, naked now, was in a dreadful state. She was trembling and shivering feverishly. Upon seeing me, she displayed a sickly but violent terror. After all, I was pale, smeared with blood, my clothes askew. Behind me, in unspeakable disorder, brazenly stripped bodies were sprawled about. During the orgy, splinters of glass had left deep bleeding cuts in two of us. A young girl was throwing up, and all of us had exploded in such wild fits of laughter at some point or other that we had wet our clothes, an armchair, or the floor. The resulting stench of blood, sperm, urine, and vomit made me almost recoil in horror, but the inhuman shriek from Marcelle's throat was far more terrifying. I must say, however, that Simone was sleeping tranquilly by now, her belly up, her hand still on her pussy, her pacified face almost smiling.

Story of the Eye

Marcelle, staggering wildly across the room with shrieks and snarls, looked at me again. She flinched back as though I were a hideous ghost in a nightmare, and she collapsed in a jeremiad of howls that grew more and more inhuman.

Astonishingly, this litany brought me to my senses. People were running up, it was inevitable. But I never for an instant dreamt of fleeing or lessening the scandal. On the contrary, I resolutely strode to the door and flung it open. What a spectacle, what joy! One can readily picture the cries of dismay, the desperate shrieks, the exaggerated threats of the parents entering the room! Criminal court, prison, the guillotine were evoked with fiery yells and spasmodic curses. Our friends themselves began howling and sobbing in a delirium of tearful screams; they sounded as if they had been set afire as live torches. Simone exulted with me.

And yet, what an atrocity! It seemed as if nothing could terminate the tragicomical frenzy of these lunatics, for Marcelle, still naked, kept gesticulating, and her agonizing shrieks of pain expressed unbearable terror and moral suffering; we watched her bite her mother's face amid arms vainly trying to subdue her.

Indeed, by bursting in, the parents managed to wipe out the last shreds of reason, and in the end, the police had to be called, with all the neighbours witnessing the outrageous scandal.

3. Marcelle's Smell

My own parents had not turned up that evening with the pack. Nevertheless, I judged it prudent to decamp and elude the wrath of an awful father, the epitome of a senile Catholic general. I entered our villa by the back door and filched a certain amount of money. Next, quite convinced they would look for me everywhere but there, I took a bath in my father's bedroom. Finally, by around ten o'clock, I was out in the open country, having left the following note on my mother's bedside table: "I beseech you not to send the police after me for I am carrying a gun, and the first bullet will be for the policeman, the second for myself."

I have never had any aptitude for what is known as striking a pose, and in this circumstance in particular, I only wished to keep my family at bay, for they relentlessly hated scandal. Still, having written the note with the greatest levity and not without laughing, I thought it might not be such a bad idea to pocket my father's revolver.

I walked along the seashore most of the night, but without getting very far from X because of all the windings of the coast. I was merely trying to soothe a violent agitation, a strange, spectral delirium in which, willy-nilly, phantasms of Simone and Marcelle took shape with gruesome expressions. Little by little, I even thought I might kill myself, and, taking the revolver in hand, I managed to lose any sense of words like hope or despair, but in my weariness, I realized that my life *had* to have some meaning all the same, and *would* have one if only certain events, defined as desirable, were to occur. I finally accepted being so extraordinarily haunted by the names *Simone* and *Marcelle*. Since it was no use laughing, I could keep going only by accepting or feigning to imagine a fantastic compromise that would confusedly link my most disconcerting moves to theirs.

I slept in a wood during the day, and at nightfall I went to Simone's place: I passed through the garden by climbing over the wall. My friend's bedroom was lit, and so I cast some pebbles through the window. A few seconds later she came down and almost wordlessly we headed towards the beach. We were delighted to see one another again. It was dark out, and from time to time I lifted her dress and took hold of her cunt, but it didn't make me come—quite the opposite. She sat down and I stretched out at her feet. I soon felt that I could not keep back my sobs, and I really cried for a long time on the sand.

"What's wrong?" asked Simone.

And she gave me a playful kick. Her foot struck the gun in my pocket and a fearful bang made us shriek at the same time. I wasn't wounded but I was up on my feet as though in a different world. Simone stood before me, frighteningly pale.

That evening we didn't even think of masturbating each other, but we remained in an endless embrace, mouth to mouth, something we had never done before.

This is how I lived for several days: Simone and I would come home late at night and sleep in her room, where I would stay locked in until the following night. Simone would bring me food, her mother, having no authority over her (the day of the scandal, she had gone for a walk the instant she heard the shrieks), accepted the situation without even trying to fathom the mystery. As for the servants, money had for some time been ensuring their devotion to Simone.

In fact, it was they who told us of the circumstances of Marcelle's confinement and even the name of the sanatorium. From the very first day, all we worried about was Marcelle: her madness, the loneliness of her body, the possibilities of getting to her, helping her to escape, perhaps. One day, when I tried to rape Simone in her bed, she brusquely slipped away:

"You're totally insane, little man," she cried, "I'm not interested—here, in a bed like this, like a housewife and mother! I'll only do it with Marcelle!"

"What are you talking about?" I asked, disappointed, but basically agreeing with her.

She came back affectionately and said in a gentle, dreamy voice:

"Listen, she won't be able to help pissing when she sees us ... doing it."

I felt a hot, enchanting liquid run down my legs, and when she was done, I got up and in turn watered her body, which she complaisantly turned to the unchaste and faintly murmuring spurt on her skin. After thus flooding her cunt, I smeared come all over her face. Full of muck, she climaxed in a liberating frenzy. She deeply inhaled our pungent and happy odour: "You smell like Marcelle," she buoyantly confided after a hefty climax, her nose under my wet arse.

Obviously Simone and I were sometimes taken with a violent desire to fuck. But we no longer thought it could be done without Marcelle, whose piercing cries kept grating on our ears, for they were linked to our most violent desires. Thus it was that our sexual dream kept changing into a nightmare. Marcelle's smile, her freshness, her sobs, the sense of shame that made her redden and, painfully red, tear off her own clothes and surrender lovely blond buttocks to impure hands, impure mouths, beyond all the tragic delirium that had made her lock herself in the wardrobe to toss off with such abandon that she could not help pissing—all these things warped our desires, so that they endlessly racked us. Simone, whose conduct during the scandal had been more obscene than ever (sprawled out, she had not even covered herself, in fact she had flung her legs apart)—Simone could not forget that the unforeseen orgasm provoked by her own brazenness, by Marcelle's howls and the nakedness of her writhing limbs, had been more powerful than anything she had ever managed to picture before. And her cunt would not open to me unless Marcelle's ghost, raging, reddening, frenzied, came to make her brazenness overwhelming and far-reaching, as if the sacrilege were to render everything generally dreadful and infamous.

At any rate, the swampy regions of the cunt (nothing resembles them more than the days of flood and storm or even the suffocating gaseous eruptions of volcanoes, and they never turn active except, like storms or volcanoes, with something of catastrophe or disaster)—those heartbreaking regions, which Simone, in an abandon presaging only violence, allowed me to stare at hypnotically, were nothing for me now but the profound, subterranean empire of a Marcelle who was tormented in prison and at the mercy of nightmares. There was only one thing I understood: how utterly the orgasms ravaged the girl's face with sobs interrupted by horrible shrieks.

And Simone, for her part, no longer viewed the hot, acrid come that she caused to spurt from my cock without seeing it muck up Marcelle's mouth and cunt.

"You could smack her face with your come," she confided to me, while smearing her cunt—"till it sizzles," as she put it.

4.   A Sunspot

Other girls and boys no longer interested us. All we could think of was Marcelle, and already we childishly imagined her hanging herself, the secret burial, the funeral apparitions. Finally, one evening, after getting the precise information, we took our bicycles and pedalled off to the sanatorium where our friend was confined. In less than an hour, we had ridden the twenty kilometres separating us from a sort of castle within a walled park on an isolated cliff overlooking the sea. We had learned that Marcelle was in Room 8, but obviously we would have to get inside the building to find her. Now all we could hope for was to climb in her window after sawing through the bars, and we were at a loss how to identify her window among thirty others, when our attention was drawn to a strange apparition. We had scaled the wall and were now in the park, among trees buffeted by a violent wind, when we spied a second-storey window opening and a shadow holding a sheet and fastening it to one of the bars. The sheet promptly smacked in the gusts, and the window was shut before we could recognize the shadow.

It is hard to imagine the harrowing racket of that vast white sheet caught in the squall. It greatly outroared the fury of the sea or the wind in the trees. That was the first time I saw Simone racked by anything but her own lewdness: she huddled against me with a beating heart and gaped at the huge phantom raging in the night as though dementia itself had hoisted its colours on this lugubrious château.

We were motionless, Simone cowering in my arms and I half-haggard, when all at once the wind seemed to tatter the clouds, and the moon, with a revealing clarity, poured sudden light on something so bizarre and so excruciating for us that an abrupt, violent sob choked up in Simone's throat: at the centre of the sheet flapping and banging in the wind, a broad wet stain glowed in the translucent moonlight. . . .

A few seconds later, new black clouds plunged everything into darkness, but I stayed on my feet, suffocating, feeling my hair in the wind, and weeping wretchedly, like Simone herself, who had collapsed in the grass, and for the first time, her body was quaking with huge, childlike sobs.

It was our unfortunate friend, no doubt about it, it was Marcelle who had opened that lightless window, Marcelle who had tied that stunning signal of distress to the bars of her prison. She had obviously tossed off in bed with such a disorder of her senses that she had entirely inundated herself, and it was then that we saw her hang the sheet from the window to let it dry.

As for myself, I was at a loss about what to do in such a park, with that bogus *château de plaisance* and its repulsively barred windows. I walked around the building, leaving Simone upset and sprawling on the grass. I had no practical goal, I just wanted to take a breath of air by myself. But then, on the side of the château, I stumbled upon an unbarred open window on the ground floor; I felt for the gun in my pocket and I entered cautiously: it was a very ordinary drawing-room. An electric flashlight helped me to reach an antechamber; then a stairway. I could not distinguish anything, I did not get anywhere, the rooms were not numbered. Besides, I was incapable of understanding anything, as though I were under a spell: at that moment, I could not even understand why I had the idea of removing my trousers and continuing that anguishing exploration only in my shirt. And yet I stripped off my clothes, piece by piece, leaving them on a chair, keeping only my shoes on. With a flashlight in my left hand and the revolver in my right hand, I wandered aimlessly, haphazardly. A rustle made me switch off my lamp quickly. I stood motionless, whiling away the time by listening to my erratic breath. Long, anxious minutes wore by without my hearing any more noise, and so I flashed my light back on, but a faint cry sent me fleeing so swiftly that I forgot my clothes on the chair.

I sensed I was being followed: so I hurriedly climbed out through the window and hid in a garden lane; but no sooner had I turned to observe what might be happening in the château than I spied a naked woman in the window frame; she jumped into the park as I had done and ran off towards a thorn bush.

Nothing was more bizarre for me in those utterly thrilling moments than my nudity against the wind on the path of that unknown garden. It was as if I had left the earth, especially because the squall was as violent as ever, but warm enough to suggest a brutal entreaty. I did not know what to do with the gun which I still held in my hand, for I had no pockets left; by charging after the woman who had run past me unrecognized, I would obviously be hunting her down to kill her. The roar of the wrathful elements, the raging of the trees and the sheet, also helped to prevent me from discerning anything distinct in my will or in my gestures.

All at once, I halted, out of breath: I had reached the bushes where the shadow had disappeared. Excited by my revolver, I began looking about, when suddenly it seemed as if all reality were tearing apart: a hand, moistened by saliva, had grabbed my cock and was rubbing it, a slobbering, burning kiss was planted on the root of my arse, the naked chest and legs of a woman pressed against my legs with an orgasmic jolt. I scarcely had time to spin around when my come burst in the face of my wonderful Simone: clutching my revolver, I was swept up by a thrill as violent as the storm, my teeth chattered and my lips foamed, with twisted arms I gripped my gun convulsively, and, willy-nilly, three blind, horrifying shots were fired in the direction of the château.

Drunk and limp, Simone and I had fled from one another and raced across the park like dogs; the squall was far too wild now for the gunshots to awake any of the sleeping tenants in the château, even if the bangs had been audible inside. But when we instinctively looked up at Marcelle's window above the sheet slamming in the wind, we were greatly surprised to see that one of the bullets had left a star-shaped crack in one of the panes. The window shook, opened, and the shadow appeared a second time.

Dumbstruck, as though about to see Marcelle bleed and fall dead in the windowframe, we remained standing under the strange, nearly motionless apparition. Because of the furious wind, we were incapable of even making ourselves heard.

"What did you do with your clothes?" I asked Simone an instant later. She said she had been looking for me and, unable to track me down, she had finally gone to search the interior of the château; but before clambering through the window, she had undressed, thinking she "would feel more free". And when she had come back out after me, terrified by me, she found that the wind had carried off her dress. Meanwhile, she kept observing Marcelle, and it never crossed her mind to ask me why *I* was naked.

The girl in the window disappeared. A moment that seemed unending crawled by: she switched on the light in her room. Finally, she came back to breathe the open air and gaze at the ocean. Her sleek, pallid hair was caught in the wind, we could make out her features: she had not changed, but now there was something wild in her eyes, something restless, contrasting with the still childlike simplicity of her features. She looked thirteen rather than sixteen. Under her nightgown, we could distinguish her thin but full body, firm, unobtrusive, and as beautiful as her fixed stare.

When she finally caught sight of us, the surprise seemed to restore life to her face. She called, but we couldn't hear. We beckoned. She blushed up to her ears. Simone, weeping almost, while I lovingly caressed her forehead, sent her kisses, to which she responded without smiling. Next, Simone ran her hand down her belly to her pubic hair. Marcelle imitated her, and poising one foot on the sill, she exposed a leg sheathed in a white silk stocking almost up to her blond cunt. Curiously, she was wearing a white belt and white stockings, whereas black-haired Simone, whose cunt was in my hand, was wearing a black belt and black stockings.

Meanwhile, the two girls were masturbating with terse, brusque gestures, face to face in the howling night. They were nearly motionless, and tense, and their eyes gaped with unrestrained joy. But soon, some invisible monstrosity appeared to be pulling Marcelle away from the bars, though her left hand clutched them with all her might. We saw her tumble back into her delirium. And all that remained before us was an empty, glowing window, a rectangular hole piercing the opaque night, showing our aching eyes a world composed of lightning and dawn.

5. A Trickle of Blood

Urine is deeply associated for me with saltpetre; and lightning, I don't know why, with an antique chamber pot of unglazed earthenware, lying abandoned one rainy autumn day on the zinc roof of a provincial wash house. Since that first night at the sanatorium, those wrenching images were closely knit, in the obscurest part of my brain, with the cunt and the drawn and dismal expression I had sometimes caught on Marcelle's face. But then, this chaotic and dreadful landscape of my imagination was suddenly inundated by a stream of light and blood, for Marcelle could come only by drenching herself, not with blood, but with a spurt of urine that was limpid and even illuminated for me, at first violent and jerky like hiccups, then free and relaxed and coinciding with an outburst of superhuman happiness. It is not astonishing that the bleakest and most leprous aspects of a dream are merely an urging in that direction, an obstinate waiting for total joy, like the vision of that glowing hole, the empty window, for example, at the very moment when Marcelle lay sprawling on the floor, endlessly inundating it.

But that day, in the rainless tempest, Simone and I, our clothing lost, were forced to leave the château, fleeing like animals through the hostile darkness, our imaginations haunted by the despondency that was bound to take hold of Marcelle again, making the wretched inmate almost an embodiment of the fury and terror that kept driving our bodies to endless debauchery. We soon found our bicycles and could offer one another the irritating and theoretically unclean sight of a naked though shod body on a machine. We pedalled rapidly, without laughing or speaking, peculiarly satisfied with our mutual presence, akin to one another in the common isolation of lewdness, weariness, and absurdity.

Yet we were both literally perishing of fatigue. In the middle of a slope, Simone halted, saying she had the shivers. Our faces, backs, and legs were bathed in sweat, and we vainly ran our hands over one another, over the various parts of our soaked and burning bodies; despite a more and more vigorous massage, she was all trembling flesh and chattering teeth. I stripped off one of her stockings to wipe her body, which gave out a hot odour recalling the beds of sickness or of debauchery. Little by little, however, she came around to a more bearable state, and finally she offered me her lips as a token of gratitude.

I was still extremely agitated. We had ten more kilometres to go, and in the state we were in, we obviously had to reach X by dawn. I could barely keep upright and despaired of ever reaching the end of this ride through the impossible. We had abandoned the real world, the one made up solely of dressed people, and the time elapsed since then was already so remote as to seem almost beyond reach. Our personal hallucination now developed as boundlessly as perhaps the total nightmare of human society, for instance, with earth, sky, and atmosphere.

A leather seat clung to Simone's bare cunt, which was inevitably jerked by the legs pumping up and down on the spinning pedals. Furthermore, the rear wheel vanished indefinitely to my eyes, not only in the bicycle fork but virtually in the crevice of the cyclist's naked bottom: the rapid whirling of the dusty tire was also directly comparable to both the thirst in my throat and the erection of my penis, destined to plunge into the depths of the cunt sticking to the bicycle seat. The wind had died down somewhat, and part of the starry sky was visible. And it struck me that death was the sole outcome of my erection, and if Simone and I were killed, then the universe of our unbearable personal vision was certain to be replaced by the pure stars, fully unrelated to any external gazes and realizing in a cold state, without human delays or detours, something that strikes me as the goal of my sexual licentiousness: a geometric incandescence (among other things, the coinciding point of life and death, being and nothingness), perfectly fulgurating.

Yet these images were, of course, tied to the contradiction of a prolonged state of exhaustion and an absurd rigidity of my penis. Now it was difficult for Simone to see this rigidity, partly because of the darkness, and partly because of the swift rising of my left leg, which kept hiding my stiffness by turning the pedal. Yet I felt I could see her eyes, aglow in the darkness, peer back constantly, no matter how fatigued, at this breaking point of my body, and I realized she was tossing off more and more violently on the seat, which was pincered between her buttocks. Like myself, she had not yet drained the tempest evoked by the shamelessness of her cunt, and at times she let out husky moans; she was literally torn away by joy, and her nude body was hurled upon an embankment with an awful scraping of steel on the pebbles and a piercing shriek.

I found her inert, her head hanging down, a thin trickle of blood running from the corner of her mouth. Horrified to the limit of my strength, I pulled up one arm, but it fell back inert. I threw myself upon the lifeless body, trembling with fear, and as I clutched it in an embrace, I was overcome with bloody spasms, my lower lip drooling and my teeth bared like a leering moron.

Meanwhile, Simone was slowly coming to: her arm touched me in an involuntary movement, and I quickly returned from the torpor overwhelming me after I had besmirched what I thought was a corpse. No injury, no bruise marked the body, which was still clad in the garter belt and a single stocking. I took her in my arms and carried her down the road, heedless of my fatigue; I walked as fast as I could because the day was just breaking, but only a superhuman effort allowed me to reach the villa and happily put my marvellous friend alive into her very own bed.

The sweat was pouring from my face and all over my body, my eyes were bloody and swollen, my ears deafened, my teeth chattering, my temples and my heart drumming away. But since I had just rescued the person I loved most in the world, and since I thought we would soon be seeing Marcelle, I lay down next to Simone's body just as I was, soaked and full of coagulated dust, and soon I drifted off into vague nightmares.

6. Simone

One of the most peaceful eras of my life was the period following Simone's minor accident, which only left her ill. Whenever her mother came, I would step into the bathroom. Usually, I took advantage of these moments to piss or even bathe; the first time the woman tried to enter, she was immediately stopped by her daughter:

"Don't go in," she said, "there's a naked man in there."

Each time, however, the mother was dismissed before long, and I would take my place again in a chair next to the sickbed. I smoked cigarettes, went through newspapers, and if there were any items about crime or violence, I would read them aloud. From time to time, I would carry a feverish Simone to the bathroom to help her pee, and then I would carefully wash her on the bidet. She was extremely weak and naturally I never stroked her seriously; but nevertheless, she soon delighted in having me throw eggs into the toilet bowl, hard-boiled eggs, which sank, and shells sucked out in various degrees to obtain varying levels of immersion. She would sit for a long time, gazing at the eggs. Then she would settle on the toilet to view them under her cunt between the parted thighs; and finally, she would have me flush the bowl.

Another game was to crack a fresh egg on the edge of the bidet and empty it under her: sometimes she would piss on it, sometimes she made me strip naked and swallow the raw egg from the bottom of the bidet. She did promise that as soon as she was well again, she would do the same for me and also for Marcelle.

At that time, we imagined Marcelle, with her dress tucked up, but her body covered and her feet shod: we would put her in a bath tub half filled with fresh eggs, and she would pee while crushing them. Simone also day-dreamed about my holding Marcelle, this time with nothing on but her garter-belt and stockings, her cunt aloft, her legs bent, and her head down; Simone herself, in a bathrobe drenched in hot water and thus clinging to her body but exposing her bosom, would then get up on a white enamelled chair with a cork seat. I would arouse her breasts from a distance by lifting the tips on the heated barrel of a long service revolver that had been loaded and just fired (first of all, this would shake us up, and secondly, it would give the barrel a pungent smell of powder). At the same time, she would pour a jar of dazzling white *crème fraîche* on Marcelle's grey anus, and she would also urinate freely in her robe or, if the robe were ajar, on Marcelle's back or head, while I could piss on Marcelle from the other side (I would certainly piss on her breasts). Furthermore, Marcelle herself could fully inundate me if she liked, for while I held her up, her thighs would be gripping my neck. And she could also stick my cock in her mouth, and what not.

It was after such dreams that Simone would ask me to bed her down on blankets by the toilet, and she would rest her head on the rim of the bowl and fix her *wide eyes* on the *white eggs*. I myself settled comfortably next to her so that our cheeks and temples might touch. We were calmed by the long contemplation. The gulping gurgle of the flushing water always amused Simone, making her forget her obsession and ultimately restoring her high spirits.

At last, one day at six, when the oblique sunshine was directly lighting the bathroom, a half-sucked egg was suddenly invaded by the water, and after filling up with a bizarre noise, it was shipwrecked before our very eyes. This incident was so extraordinarily meaningful to Simone that her body tautened and she had a long climax, virtually drinking my left eye between her lips. Then, without leaving the eye, which was sucked as obstinately as a breast, she sat down, wrenching my head toward her on the seat, and she pissed noisily on the bobbing eggs with total vigour and satisfaction.

By then she could be regarded as cured, and she demonstrated her joy by speaking to me at length about various intimate things, whereas ordinarily she never spoke about herself or me. Smiling, she admitted that an instant ago, she had felt a strong urge to relieve herself completely, but had held back for the sake of greater pleasure. Truly, the urge bloated her belly and particularly made her cunt swell up like a ripe fruit; and when I passed my hand under the sheets and her cunt gripped it firm and tight, she remarked that she was still in the same state and that it was inordinately pleasant. Upon my asking what the word *urinate* reminded her of, she replied: *terminate,* the eyes, with a razor, something red, the sun. And *egg?* A calf's eye, because of the colour of the head (the calf's head) and also because the white of the egg was the white of the eye, and the yolk the eyeball. The eye, she said, was egg-shaped. She asked me to promise that when we could go outdoors, I would fling eggs into the sunny air and break them with shots from my gun, and when I replied that it was out of the question, she talked on and on, trying to reason me into it. She played gaily with words, speaking about *broken eggs,* and then *broken eyes,* and her arguments became more and more unreasonable.

She added that, for her, the smell of the arse was the smell of powder, a jet of urine a "gunshot seen as a light"; each of her buttocks was a peeled hard-boiled egg. We agreed to send for hot soft-boiled eggs without shells, for the toilet, and she promised that when she now sat on the seat, she would ease herself fully on those eggs. Her cunt was still in my hand and in the state she had described; and after her promise, a storm began brewing little by little in my innermost depth—I was reflecting more and more.

It is fair to say that the room of a bedridden invalid is just the right place for gradually rediscovering childhood lewdness. I gently sucked Simone's breast while waiting for the soft-boiled eggs, and she ran her fingers through my hair. Her mother was the one who brought us the eggs, but I didn't even turn around, I assumed it was a maid, and I kept on sucking the breast contentedly. Nor was I ultimately disturbed when I recognized the voice, but since she remained and I couldn't forego even one instant of my pleasure, I thought of pulling down my trousers as for a call of nature, not ostentatiously, but merely hoping she would leave and delighted at going beyond all limits. When she finally decided to walk out and vainly ponder over her dismay elsewhere, the night was already gathering, and we switched on the lamp in the bathroom. Simone settled on the toilet, and we each ate one of the hot eggs with salt. With the three that were left, I softly caressed her body, gliding them between her buttocks and thighs, then I slowly dropped them into the water one by one. Finally, after viewing them for a while, immersed, white, and still hot (this was the first time she was seeing them peeled, that is naked, drowned under her beautiful cunt), Simone continued the immersion with a plopping noise akin to that of the soft-boiled eggs.

But I ought to say that nothing of the sort ever happened between us again, and, *with one exception,* no further eggs ever came up in our conversations; nevertheless, if we chanced to notice one or more, we could not help reddening when our eyes met in a silent and murky interrogation.

At any rate, it will be shown by the end of this tale, that this interrogation was not to remain without an answer indefinitely, and above all, that this unexpected answer is necessary for measuring the immensity of the void that yawned before us, without our knowledge, during our singular entertainments with the eggs.

7. Marcelle

By a sort of shared modesty, Simone and I had always avoided talking about the most important objects of our obsessions. That was why the word *egg* was dropped from our vocabulary, and we never spoke about the kind of interest we had in one another, even less about what Marcelle meant to us. We spent all of Simone's illness in a bedroom, looking forward to when we could go back to Marcelle, as nervously as we had once waited for the end of the last lesson in school, and so all we talked about was the day we would return to the château. I had prepared a small cord, a thick, knotted rope, and a hacksaw, all of which Simone examined with the keenest interest, peering attentively at each knot and section of the rope. I also managed to find the bicycles, which I had concealed in a thicket the day of our tumble, and I meticulously oiled the various

parts, the gears, ball bearings, sprockets, etc. I then attached a pair
of foot-rests to my own bicycle so that I could seat one of the girls
behind . Nothing could be easier, at least for the time being, than to
have Marcelle living in Simone's room secretly like myself. We
would simply be forced to share the bed (and we would inevitably
have to use the same bathtub, etc.).

But a good six weeks passed before Simone could pedal after me
reasonably well to the sanatorium. Like the previous time, we left
at night: in fact, I still kept out of sight during the day, and this time
there was certainly every reason for remaining inconspicuous. I
was in a hurry to arrive at the place that I dimly regarded as a
"haunted castle," due to the association of the words *sanatorium*
and *castle,* and also the memory of the phantom sheet and the
thought of the lunatics in a huge silent dwelling at night. But now,
to my surprise, even though I was ill at ease anywhere in the world,
I felt at bottom as if I were going home. And that was indeed my
impression when we jumped over the park wall and saw the huge
building stretching out ahead beyond the trees: only Marcelle's
window was still aglow and wide open. Taking some pebbles from
a lane, we threw them into her chamber and they promptly
summoned the girl, who quickly recognized us and obeyed our
gesture of putting a finger on our lips. But of course we also held
up the knotted rope to let her understand what we were doing this
time. I hurled the cord up to her with the aid of a stone, and she
threw it back after looping it around a bar. There were no
difficulties, the big rope was hoisted by Marcelle and fastened to
the bar, and I scrambled all the way up.

   Marcelle flinched when I tried to kiss her. She merely watched
me very attentively as I started filing away at a bar. Since she only
had a bathrobe on, I softly told her to get dressed so she could come
with us. She simply turned her back to pull flesh-coloured
stockings over her legs, securing them on a belt of bright red
ribbons that brought out a rump with a perfect shape and an
exceptionally fine skin. I continued filing, bathed in sweat because
of both my effort and what I saw. Her back still towards me,

Marcelle pulled a blouse over long, flat hips, whose straight lines were admirably terminated by the buttocks when she had one foot on a chair. She did not slip on any panties, only a pleated grey woollen skirt and a sweater with very tiny black, white, and red checks. After stepping into flat-heeled shoes, she came over to the window and sat down close enough to me so that my one hand could caress her head, her lovely short hair, so sleek and so blond that it actually looked pale. She gazed at me affectionately and seemed touched by my wordless joy at seeing her.

"Now we can get married, can't we?" she finally said, gradually won over. "It's very bad here, we suffer. . . ."

At that point, I would never have dreamt for even an instant that I could do anything but devote the rest of my life to such an unreal apparition. She let me give her a long kiss on her forehead and her eyes, and when one of her hands happened to touch my leg, she looked at me wide-eyed, but before withdrawing her hand, she ran it over my clothes absent-mindedly.

After long work, I succeeded in cutting through the horrid bar. I pulled it aside with all my strength, which left enough space for her to squeeze through. She did so, and I helped her descend, climbing down underneath, which forced me to see the top of her thigh and even to touch it when I supported her. Reaching the ground, she snuggled in my arms and kissed my mouth with all her strength, while Simone, sitting at our feet, her eyes wet with tears, flung her hands around Marcelle's legs, hugging her knees and thighs. At first, she only rubbed her cheek against the thigh, but then, unable to restrain a huge surge of joy, she finally yanked the body apart, pressing her lips to the cunt, which she greedily devoured.

However, Simone and I realized that Marcelle grasped absolutely nothing of what was going on and she was actually incapable of telling one situation from another. Thus she smiled, imagining how aghast the director of the "haunted castle" would be to see her strolling through the garden with her husband. Also, she was scarcely aware of Simone's existence; mirthfully, she at times mistook her for a wolf because of her black hair, her silence, and because Simone's head was docilely rubbing Marcelle's thigh, like a dog nuzzling his master's leg. Nonetheless, when I spoke to Marcelle about the "haunted castle," she did not ask me to explain; she understood that this was the building where she had been wickedly locked up. And whenever she thought of it, her terror pulled her away from me as though she had seen something pass through the trees. I watched her uneasily, and since my face was already hard and sombre, I too frightened her, and almost at the same instant she asked me to protect her *when the Cardinal returned*.

We were lying in the moonlight by the edge of a forest. We wanted to rest a while during our trip back and we especially wanted to embrace and stare at Marcelle.

"But who is the Cardinal?" Simone asked her.

"The man who locked me in the wardrobe," said Marcelle.

"But why is he a cardinal?" I cried.

She replied: "Because he is the priest of the guillotine."

I now recalled Marcelle's dreadful fear when she left the wardrobe, and particularly two details: I had been wearing a blinding red carnival novelty, a Jacobine liberty cap; furthermore, because of the deep cuts in a girl I had raped, my face, clothes, hands—all parts of me were stained with blood.

Thus, in her terror, Marcelle confused a cardinal, a priest of the guillotine, with the blood-smeared executioner wearing a liberty cap: a bizarre overlapping of piety and abomination for priests explained the confusion, which, for me, had remained attached to both my hard reality and the horror continually aroused by the compulsiveness of my actions.

8. The Open Eyes of the Dead Woman

For a moment, I was totally helpless after this unexpected discovery; and so was Simone. Marcelle was now half asleep in my arms, so that we didn't know what to do. Her dress was pulled up, exposing the grey pussy between red ribbons at the end of long thighs, and it had thereby become an extraordinary hallucination in a world so frail that a mere breath might have changed us into light. We didn't dare budge, and all we desired was for that unreal immobility to last as long as possible, and for Marcelle to fall sound asleep.

My mind reeled in some kind of exhausting vertigo, and I don't know what the outcome would have been if Simone, whose worried gaze was darting between my eyes and Marcelle's nudity, had not made a sudden, gentle movement: she opened her thighs, saying in a blank voice that she couldn't hold back any longer.

She soaked her dress in a long convulsion that fully denuded her and promptly made me spurt a wave of semen in my clothes.

I stretched out in the grass, my skull on a large, flat rock and my eyes staring straight up at the Milky Way, that strange breach of astral sperm and heavenly urine across the cranial vault formed by the ring of constellations: that open crack at the summit of the sky, apparently made of ammoniacal vapours shining in the immensity (in empty space, where they burst forth absurdly like a rooster's crow in total silence), a broken egg, a broken eye, or my own dazzled skull weighing down the rock, bouncing symmetrical images back to infinity. The nauseating crow of a rooster in particular coincided with my own life, that is to say, now, the Cardinal, because of the crack, the red colour, the discordant shrieks he provoked in the wardrobe, and also because one cuts the throats of roosters.

To others, the universe seems decent because decent people have gelded eyes. That is why they fear lewdness. They are never frightened by the crowing of a rooster or when strolling under a starry heaven. In general, people savour the "pleasures of the flesh" only on condition that they be insipid.

But as of then, no doubt existed for me: I did not care for what is known as "pleasures of the flesh" because they really are insipid; I cared only for what is classified as "dirty". On the other hand, I was not even satisfied with the usual debauchery, because the only thing it dirties is debauchery itself, while, in some way or other, anything sublime and perfectly pure is left intact by it. My kind of debauchery soils not only my body and my thoughts, but also anything I may conceive in its course, that is to say, the vast starry universe, which merely serves as a backdrop.

I associate the moon with the vaginal blood of mothers, sisters, that is, the menstrua with their sickening stench. ...

I loved Marcelle without mourning her. If she died, then it was my fault. If I had nightmares, if I sometimes locked myself up in a cellar for hours at a time precisely because I was thinking about

Marcelle, I would nevertheless still be prepared to start all over again, for instance by ducking her hair, head down, in a toilet bowl. But since she is dead, I have nothing left but certain catastrophes that bring me to her at times when I least expect it. Otherwise, I cannot possibly perceive the least kinship now between the dead girl and myself, which makes most of my days inevitably dreary.

I will merely report here that Marcelle hanged herself after a dreadful incident. She recognized the huge bridal wardrobe, and her teeth started chattering: she instantly realized upon looking at me that *I* was the man she called the Cardinal, and when she began shrieking, there was no other way for me to stop that desperate howling than to leave the room. By the time Simone and I returned she was hanging inside the wardrobe. ...

I cut the rope, but she was quite dead. We laid her out on the carpet. Simone saw I was getting a hard-on and she started tossing me off. I too stretched out on the carpet. It was impossible to do otherwise; Simone was still a virgin, and I fucked her for the first time, next to the corpse. It was very painful for both of us, but we were glad precisely because it *was* painful. Simone stood up and gazed at the corpse. Marcelle had become a total stranger, and in fact, so had Simone at that moment. I no longer cared at all for either Simone or Marcelle. Even if someone had told me it was I who had just died, I would not even have been astonished, so alien were these events to me. I observed Simone, and, as I precisely recall, my only pleasure was in the smutty things Simone was doing, for the corpse was very irritating to her, as though she could not bear the thought that this creature, so similar to her, could not feel her anymore. The open eyes were more irritating than anything else. Even when Simone drenched the face, those eyes, extraordinarily, did not close. We were perfectly calm, all *three* of us, and that was the most hopeless part of it. Any boredom in the world is linked, for me, to that moment and, above all, to an obstacle as ridiculous as death. But that won't prevent me from thinking back to that time with no revulsion and even with a sense of complicity. Basically, the lack of excitement made everything far more absurd, and thus Marcelle was closer to me dead than in her lifetime, inasmuch as absurd existence, so I imagine, has all the prerogatives.

As for the fact that Simone dared to piss on the corpse, whether in boredom or, at worst, in irritation: it mainly goes to prove how impossible it was for us to understand what was happening, and of course, it is no more understandable today than it was then. Simone, being truly incapable of conceiving death such as one normally considers it, was frightened and furious, but in no way awe-struck. Marcelle belonged to us so deeply in our isolation that we could not see her as just another corpse. Nothing about her death could be measured by a common standard, and the contradictory impulses overtaking us in this circumstance neutralized one another, leaving us blind and, as it were, very remote from anything we touched, in a world where gestures have no carrying power, like voices in a space that is absolutely soundless.

9. Lewd Animals

To avoid the bother of a police investigation, we instantly took off
for Spain, where Simone was counting on our disappearing with
the help of a fabulously rich Englishman, who had offered to
support her and would be more likely than anyone else to show
interest in our plight.

The villa was abandoned in the middle of the night. We had no
trouble stealing a boat, reaching an obscure point on the Spanish
coast, and burning the vessel with the aid of two drums of petrol
that we had taken along, as a precautionary measure, from the
garage of the villa. Simone left me concealed in a wood during the
day and went to look for the Englishman in San Sebastian. She
only came back at nightfall, but driving a magnificent automobile,

with suitcases full of linen and rich clothing.

Simone said that Sir Edmund would join us in Madrid and that all day long he had been plying her with the most detailed questions about Marcelle's death, making her draw diagrams and sketches. Finally he had told a servant to buy a wax mannequin with a blonde wig; he had then laid the figure out on the floor and asked Simone to urinate on its face, on the open eyes, in the same position as she had urinated on the eyes of the corpse: during all that time, Sir Edmund had not even touched her.

However, there had been a great change in Simone after Marcelle's suicide—she kept staring into space all the time, looking as if she belonged to something other than the terrestrial world, where almost everything bored her; or if she *was* still attached to this world, then purely by way of orgasms, which were rare but incomparably more violent than before. These orgasms were as different from normal climaxes as, say, the mirth of savage Africans from that of Occidentals. In fact, though the savages may sometimes laugh as moderately as whites, they also have long-lasting spasms, with all parts of the body in violent release, and they go whirling willy-nilly, flailing their arms about wildly, shaking their bellies, necks, and chests, and chortling and gulping horribly. As for Simone, she would first open uncertain eyes, at some lewd and dismal sight. . . .

For example, Sir Edmund had a cramped, windowless pigsty, where one day he locked up a petite and luscious streetwalker from Madrid; wearing only cami-knickers, she collapsed in a pool of liquid manure under the bellies of the grunting swine. Once the door was shut, Simone had me fuck her again and again in front of that door, with her arse in the mud, under a fine drizzle of rain, while Sir Edmund tossed off.

Gasping and slipping away from me, Simone grabbed her behind in both hands and threw back her head, which banged violently against the ground; she tensed breathlessly for a few seconds, pulling with all her might on the fingernails buried in her buttocks, then tore herself away at one swoop and thrashed about on the ground like a headless chicken, hurting herself with a terrible bang on the door fittings. Sir Edmund gave her his wrist to bite on and allay the spasm that kept shaking her, and I saw that her face was smeared with saliva and blood.

After these huge fits, she always came to nestle in my arms; she settled her little bottom comfortably in my large hands and remained there for a long time without moving or speaking, huddled like a little girl, but always sombre.

Sir Edmund deployed his ingenuity at providing us with obscene spectacles at random, but Simone still preferred bullfights. There were actually three things about bullfights that fascinated her: the first, when the bull comes hurtling out of the bullpen like a big rat; the second, when its horns plunge all the way into the flank of a mare; the third, when that ludicrous, raw-boned mare gallops across the arena, lashing out unseasonably and dragging a huge, vile bundle of bowels between her thighs in the most dreadful wan colours, a pearly white, pink, and grey. Simone's heart throbbed fastest when the exploding bladder dropped its mass of mare's urine on the sand in one quick plop.

She was on tenterhooks from start to finish at the bullfight, in terror (which of course mainly expressed a violent desire) at the thought of seeing the toreador hurled up by one of the monstrous lunges of the horns when the bull made its endless, blindly raging dashes at the void of coloured cloths. And there is something else I ought to say: when the bull makes its quick, brutal, thrusts over and over again into the matador's cape, barely grazing the erect line of the body, any spectator has that feeling of total and repeated lunging typical of the game of coitus. The utter nearness of death is also felt in the same way. But these series of prodigious passes are rare. Thus, each time they occur, they unleash a veritable delirium in the arena, and it is well known that at such thrilling instants the women come by merely rubbing their thighs together.

Apropos bullfights, Sir Edmund once told Simone that until quite recently, certain virile Spaniards, mostly occasional amateur toreadors, used to ask the caretaker of the arena to bring them the fresh, roasted balls of one of the first bulls to be killed. They received them at their seats, in the front row of the arena, and ate them while watching the killing of the next few bulls. Simone took a keen interest in this tale, and since we were attending the first major bullfight of the year that Sunday, she begged Sir Edmund to get her the balls of the first bull, but added one condition: they had to be raw.

"I say," objected Sir Edmund, "whatever do you want with raw balls? You certainly don't intend to eat raw balls now, do you?"

"I want to have them before me on a plate," concluded Simone.

10. Granero's Eye

On May 7, 1922, the toreadors La Rosa, Lalanda, and Granero were to fight in the arena of Madrid; the last two were renowned as the best matadors in Spain, and Granero was generally considered superior to Lalanda. He had only just turned twenty, yet he was already extremely popular, being handsome, tall and of a still childlike simplicity. Simone had been deeply interested in his story, and, exceptionally, had shown genuine pleasure when Sir Edmund announced that the celebrated bull-killer had agreed to dine with us the evening of the fight.

Granero stood out from the rest of the matadors because there was nothing of the butcher about him; he looked more like a very manly Prince Charming with a perfectly elegant figure. In this respect, the matador's costume is quite expressive, for it safeguards the straight line shooting up so rigid and erect every time the lunging bull grazes the body and because the pants so tightly sheathe the behind. A bright red cloth and a brilliant sword (before the dying bull whose hide steams with sweat and blood) complete the metamorphosis, bringing out the most captivating feature of the game. One must also bear in mind the typically torrid Spanish sky, which never has the colour or harshness one imagines: it is just perfectly sunny with a dazzling but mellow sheen, hot, turbid, at times even unreal when the combined intensities of light and heat suggest the freedom of the senses.

Now this extreme unreality of the solar blaze was so closely attached to everything happening around me during the bullfight on May 7, that the only objects I have ever carefully preserved are a round paper fan, half yellow, half blue, that Simone had that day, and a small illustrated brochure with a description of all the circumstances and a few photographs. Later on, during an embarkment, the small valise containing those two souvenirs tumbled into the sea, and was fished out by an Arab with a long pole, which is why the objects are in such a bad state. But I need them to fix that event to the earthly soil, to a geographic point and a precise date, an event that my imagination compulsively pictures as a simple vision of solar deliquescence.

The first bull, the one whose balls Simone looked forward to having served raw on a plate, was a kind of black monster, who shot out of the pen so quickly that despite all efforts and all shouts, he disembowelled three horses in a row before an orderly fight could take place; one horse and rider were hurled aloft together, loudly crashing down behind the horns. But when Granero faced the bull, the combat was launched with brio, proceeding amid a frenzy of cheers. The young man sent the furious beast racing around him in his pink cape; each time, his body was lifted by a sort of spiralling jet, and he just barely eluded a frightful impact. In the end, the death of the solar monster was performed cleanly, with the beast blinded by the scrap of red cloth, the sword deep in the blood-smeared body. An incredible ovation resounded as the bull staggered to its knees with the uncertainty of a drunkard, collapsed with its legs sticking up, and died.

Simone, who sat between Sir Edmund and myself, witnessed the killing with an exhilaration at least equal to mine, and she refused to sit down again when the interminable acclamation for the young man was over. She took my hand wordlessly and led me to an outer courtyard of the filthy arena, where the stench of equine and human urine was suffocating because of the great heat. I grabbed Simone's cunt, and she seized my furious cock through my trousers. We stepped into a stinking shithouse, where sordid flies whirled about in a sunbeam. Standing here, I exposed Simone's cunt, and into her blood-red, slobbery flesh I stuck my fingers, then my penis, which entered that cavern of blood while I tossed off her arse, thrusting my bony middle finger deep inside. At the same time, the roofs of our mouths cleaved together in a storm of saliva.

A bull's orgasm is not more powerful than the one that wrenched through our loins to tear us to shreds, though without shaking my thick penis out of that stuffed vulva, which was gorged with come.

Our hearts were still booming in our chests, which were equally burning and equally lusting to press stark naked against wet unslaked hands, and Simone's cunt was still as greedy as before and my cock stubbornly rigid, as we returned to the first row of the arena. But when we arrived at our places next to Sir Edmund, there, in broad sunlight, on Simone's seat, lay a white dish containing two peeled balls, glands the size and shape of eggs, and of a pearly whiteness, faintly bloodshot, like the globe of an eye: they had just been removed from the first bull, a black-haired creature, into whose body Granero had plunged his sword.

"Here are the raw balls," Sir Edmund said to Simone in his British accent.

Simone was already kneeling before the plate, peering at it in absorbed interest, but in something of a quandary. It seemed she wanted to do something but didn't know how to go about it, which exasperated her. I picked up the dish to let her sit down, but she grabbed it away from me with a categorical "no" and returned it to the stone seat.

Sir Edmund and I were growing annoyed at being the focus of our neighbours' attention just when the bullfight was slackening. I leaned over and whispered to Simone, asking what had got into her.

"Idiot!" she replied. "Can't you see I want to sit on the plate, and all these people watching!"

"That's absolutely out of the question," I rejoined, "sit down."

At the same time, I took away the dish and made her sit, and I stared at her to let her know that I understood, that I remembered the dish of milk, and that this renewed desire was unsettling me. From that moment on, neither of us could keep from fidgeting, and this state of malaise was contagious enough to affect Sir Edmund. I ought to say that the fight had become boring, unpugnacious bulls were facing matadors who didn't know what to do next; and to top it off, since Simone had demanded seats in the sun, we were trapped in something like an immense vapour of light and muggy heat, which parched our throats as it bore down upon us.

It really was totally out of the question for Simone to lift her dress and place her bare behind in the dish of raw balls. All she could do was hold the dish in her lap. I told her I would like to fuck her again before Granero returned to fight the fourth bull, but she refused, and she sat there, keenly involved, despite everything, in the disembowelments of horses, followed, as she childishly put it, by "death and destruction", namely the cataract of bowels.

Little by little, the sun's radiance sucked us into an unreality that fitted our malaise—the wordless and powerless desire to explode and get up off our behinds. We grimaced, because our eyes were blinded and because we were thirsty, our senses ruffled, and there was no possibility of quenching our desires. We three had managed to share in the morose dissolution that leaves no harmony between the various spasms of the body. We were so far gone that even Granero's return could not pull us out of that stupefying absorption. Besides, the bull opposite him was distrustful and seemed unresponsive; the combat went on just as drearily as before.

The events that followed were without transition or connection, not because they weren't actually related, but because my attention was so absent as to remain absolutely dissociated. In just a few seconds: first, Simone bit into one of the raw balls, to my dismay; then Granero advanced towards the bull, waving his scarlet cloth; finally, almost at once, Simone, with a blood-red face and a suffocating lewdness, uncovered her long white thighs up to her moist vulva, into which she slowly and surely fitted the second pale globule—Granero was thrown back by the bull and wedged against the balustrade; the horns struck the balustrade three times at full speed; at the third blow, one horn plunged into the right eye and through the head. A shriek of unmeasured horror coincided with a brief orgasm for Simone, who was lifted up from the stone seat only to be flung back with a bleeding nose, under a blinding sun; men instantly rushed over to haul away Granero's body, the right eye dangling from the head.

11. Under the Sun of Seville

Thus, two globes of equal size and consistency had suddenly been propelled in opposite directions at once. One, the white ball of the bull, had been thrust into the "pink and dark" cunt that Simone had bared in the crowd; the other, a human eye, had spurted from Granero's head with the same force as a bundle of innards from a belly. This coincidence, tied to death and to a sort of urinary liquefaction of the sky, first brought us back to Marcelle in a moment that was so brief and almost insubstantial, yet so uneasily vivid that I stepped forward like a sleepwalker as though about to touch *her* at eye level.

Needless to say, everything was promptly back to normal, though with blinding obsessions in the hour after Granero's death. Simone was in such a foul mood that she told Sir Edmund she wouldn't spend another day in Madrid; she was very anxious to see Seville because of its reputation as a city of pleasure.

Sir Edmund took a heady delight in satisfying the whims of "the simplest and most angelic creature ever to walk the earth," and so the next day he accompanied us to Seville, where we found an even more liquefying heat and light than in Madrid. A lavish abundance of flowers in the streets, geraniums and rose laurels, helped to put our senses on edge.

Simone walked about naked under a white dress that was flimsy enough to hint at the red garter-belt underneath and, in certain positions, even at her pussy. Furthermore, everything in this city contributed to making her radiate such sensuality that when we passed through the torrid streets, I often saw cocks stretching trousers.

Indeed, we virtually never stopped having sex. We avoided orgasms and we went sight-seeing, for this was the only way to keep from having my penis endlessly immersed in her fur. But we did take advantage of any opportunities when we were out. We would leave one convenient place with never any goal but to find another like it. An empty museum room, a stairway, a garden path lined with high bushes, an open church, deserted alleys in the evenings—we walked until we found the right place, and the instant we found it, I would open the girl's body by lifting one of her legs and shoving my cock to the bottom of her cunt in one swoop. A few moments later, I would pull my steaming member from its stable, and our promenade would continue almost aimlessly. Usually, Sir Edmund would follow at a distance in order to surprise us: he would turn purple, but he never came close. And if he masturbated, he would do it discreetly, not for caution's sake, of course, but because he never did anything unless standing isolated and almost utterly steady, with a dreadful muscular contraction.

"This is a very interesting place," he said one day in regard to a church, "it's the church of Don Juan."

"So what?" replied Simone.

"Stay here with me," Sir Edmund said to me. "And you, Simone, you ought to go round this church all by yourself."

"What an awful idea!"

Nevertheless, however awful the idea, it aroused her curiosity, and she went in by herself while we waited in the street.

Five minutes later, Simone reappeared at the threshold of the church. We were dumbstruck: not only was she guffawing her head off, but she couldn't speak or stop laughing, so that, partly by contagion, partly because of the intense light, I began laughing as hard as she, and so did Sir Edmund to a certain extent.

"Bloody girl," he said. "Can't you explain? By the by, we're laughing right over the tomb of Don Juan!"

And laughing even harder, he pointed at a large church brass at our feet. It was the tomb of the church's founder, who, the guides claimed, was Don Juan: after repenting, he had himself buried under the doorstep so that the faithful would trudge over his corpse when entering or leaving their haunt.

But now our wild laughter burst out again tenfold. In our mirth, Simone had lightly pissed down her leg, and a tiny trickle of water had landed on the brass.

We noted a further effect of her accident: the thin dress, being wet, stuck to her body, and since the cloth was now fully transparent, Simone's attractive belly and thighs were revealed with particular lewdness, a dark patch between the red ribbons of her garter belt.

"All I can do is go into the church," said Simone, a bit calmer, "it'll dry."

We burst into a larger space, where Sir Edmund and I vainly looked for the comical sight that the girl had been unable to explain. The room was relatively cool, and the light came from windows, filtering through curtains of a bright red, transparent cretonne. The ceiling was of carved woodwork, the walls were plastered but encumbered with religious gewgaws more or less gilded. The entire back wall was covered from floor to rafters by an altar and a giant Baroque retablo of gilded wood; the involved and contorted decorations conjured up India, with deep shadows and golden glows, and the whole altar at first seemed very mysterious and just right for sex. At either side of the entrance door hung two famous canvases by the painter Valdès Leal, pictures of decomposing corpses: interestingly, one of the eye sockets was being gnawed through by a rat. Yet in all these things, there was nothing funny to be found.

Quite the contrary: the whole place was sumptuous and sensuous, the play of shadows and light from the red curtains, the coolness and a strong pungent aroma of blossoming oleander, plus the dress sticking to Simone's pussy—everything was urging me to burst loose and bare that wet cunt on the floor, when I spied a pair of silk shoes at a confessional: the feet of a penitent female.

"I want to see them leave," said Simone.

She sat down before me, not far from the confessional, and all I could do was caress her neck, the line of her hair, or her shoulders with my cock. And that put her so much on edge that she told me to tuck my penis away immediately or she would rub it until I came.

I had to sit down and merely look at Simone's nakedness through the soaked cloth, at its best in the open air, when she wanted to fan her wet thighs and she uncrossed them and lifted her dress.

"You'll see," she said.

That was why I patiently waited for the key to the puzzle. After a rather long wait, a very beautiful young brunette stepped out of the confessional, her hands folded, her face pale and enraptured: with her head thrown back and her eyes white and vacant, she slowly eased across the room like an opera ghost. There was something so truly unexpected about the whole thing that I desperately squeezed my legs together to keep from laughing, when the door of the confessional opened: someone else emerged, this time a blond priest, very young, very handsome, with a long thin face and the pale eyes of a saint. His arms were crossed on his chest, and he remained on the threshold of the booth, gazing at a fixed point on the ceiling as though a celestial apparition were about to help him levitate.

The priest thus moved in the same direction as the woman, and he would probably have vanished in turn without seeing anything if Simone, to my great surprise, had not brought him up sharply. Something unbelievable had occurred to her: she greeted the visionary courteously and said she wanted to confess.

The priest, still gliding in his ecstasy, indicated the confessional with a distant gesture and reentered his tabernacle, softly closing the door without a word.

12.   Simone's Confession and Sir Edmund's Mass

One can readily imagine my stupor at watching Simone kneel down by the cabinet of the lugubrious confessor. While she confessed her sins, I waited, extremely anxious to see the outcome of such an unexpected action. I assumed this sordid creature was going to burst from his booth, pounce upon the impious girl, and flagellate her. I was even getting ready to knock the dreadful phantom down and treat him to a few kicks; but nothing of the sort happened: the booth remained closed, Simone spoke on and on through the tiny grilled window, and that was all.

I was exchanging sharply interrogative looks with Sir Edmund when things began to grow clear: Simone was slowly scratching her thigh, moving her legs apart; keeping one knee on the prayer stool, she shifted one foot to the floor, and she was exposing more and more of her legs over her stockings while still murmuring her confession. At times she even seemed to be tossing off.

I softly drew up at the side to try and see what was happening: Simone really *was* masturbating, the left part of her face was pressed against the grille near the priest's head, her limbs tensed, her thighs splayed, her fingers rummaging deep in the fur; I was able to touch her, I bared her cunt for an instant. At that moment, I distinctly heard her say:

"Father, I still have not confessed the worst sin of all."

A few seconds of silence.

"The worst sin of all is very simply that I'm tossing off while talking to you."

More seconds of whispering inside, and finally almost aloud:

"If you don't believe me, I can show you."

And indeed, Simone stood up and spread one thigh before the eye of the window while masturbating with a quick, sure hand.

"All right, priest," cried Simone, banging away at the confessional, "what are you doing in your shack there? Tossing off, too?"

But the confessional kept its peace.

"Well, then I'll open."

And Simone pulled out the door.

Inside, the visionary, standing there with lowered head, was mopping a sweat-bathed brow. The girl groped for his cock under the cassock: he didn't turn a hair. She pulled up the filthy black skirt so that the long cock stuck out, pink and hard: all he did was throw back his head with a grimace, and a hiss escaped through his teeth, but he didn't interfere with Simone, who shoved the bestiality into her mouth and took long sucks on it.

Sir Edmund and I were immobile in our stupor. For my part, I was spellbound with admiration, and I didn't know what else to do, when the enigmatic Englishman resolutely strode to the confessional and, after edging Simone aside as delicately as could be, dragged the larva out of its hole by its wrists, and flung it brutally at our feet: the vile priest lay there like a cadaver, his teeth to the ground, not uttering a cry. We promptly carried him to the vestry.

His fly was open, his cock dangling, his face livid and drenched with sweat, he didn't resist, but breathed heavily: we put him in a large wooden armchair with architectural decorations.

"*Señores,*" the wretch snivelled, "you must think I'm a hypocrite."

"No," replied Sir Edmund with a categorical intonation.

Simone asked him: "What's your name?"

"Don Aminado," he answered.

Simone slapped the sacerdotal pig, which gave him another hard-on. We stripped off all his clothes, and Simone crouched down and pissed on them like a bitch. Then she wanked and sucked the pig while I urinated in his nostrils. Finally, to top off this cold exaltation, I fucked Simone in the arse while she violently sucked his cock.

Meanwhile, Sir Edmund, contemplating the scene with his characteristic poker face, carefully inspected the room where we had found refuge. He glimpsed a tiny key hanging from a nail in the woodwork.

"What is that key for?' he asked Don Aminado.

From the expression of dread on the priest's face, Sir Edmund realized it was the key to the tabernacle.

The Englishman returned a few moments later, carrying a ciborium of twisted gold, decorated with a quantity of angels as naked as cupids. The wretched Don Aminado gaped at this receptacle of consecrated hosts on the floor, and his handsome moronic face, already contorted because Simone was flagellating his cock with her teeth and tongue, was now fully gasping and panting.

After barricading the door, Sir Edmund rummaged through the closets until he finally lit upon a large chalice, whereupon he asked us to abandon the wretch for an instant.

"Look," he explained to Simone, "the eucharistic hosts in the ciborium, and here the chalice where they put white wine."

"They smell like come," said Simone, sniffing the unleavened wafers.

"Precisely," continued Sir Edmund. "The hosts, as you see, are

nothing other than Christ's sperm in the form of small white
biscuits. And as for the wine they put in the chalice, the ecclesiastics
say it is the *blood* of Christ, but they are obviously mistaken. If they
really thought it was the blood, they would use *red* wine, but since
they employ only *white* wine, they are showing that at the bottom
of their hearts they are quite aware that this is urine."

The lucidity of this logic was so convincing that Simone and I
required no further explanation. She, armed with the chalice and I
with the ciborium, the two of us marched over to Don Aminado,
who was still inert in his armchair, faintly agitated by a slight
quiver through his body.

Simone began by slamming the base of the chalice against his
skull, which jolted him and left him utterly dazed. Then she
resumed sucking him, which provoked his ignoble rattles. After
bringing his senses to a height of fury with Sir Edmund's help and
mine, she gave him a hard shake.

"That's not all," she said in a voice that brooked no reply. "It's
time to piss."

And she struck his face again with the chalice, but at the same
time she stripped naked before him and I finger-fucked her.

Sir Edmund's gaze, fixed on the stunned eyes of the young
cleric, was so imperious that the thing went off with barely any
hitch; Don Aminado noisily poured his urine into the chalice,
which Simone held under this thick cock.

"And now, drink," commanded Sir Edmund.

The paralyzed wretch drank with a well-nigh filthy ecstasy at
one long gluttonous draft. Again Simone sucked and wanked him;
he continued gurgling desperately and revelling in it. With a
demented gesture, he bashed the sacred chamber-pot against a
wall. Four robust arms lifted him up and, with open thighs, his
body erect, and yelling like a pig being slaughtered, he spurted his
come on the hosts in the ciborium, which Simone held in front of
him while masturbating him.

13. The Legs of the Fly

We dropped the swine and he crashed to the floor. Sir Edmund, Simone, and myself were coldly animated by the same determination, together with an incredible excitement and levity. The priest lay there with a limp cock, his teeth digging into the floor with rage and shame. Now that his balls were drained, his abomination appeared to him in all its horror. He audibly sighed:

"Oh miserable sacrileges. . . ."

And muttering other incomprehensible laments.

Sir Edmund nudged him with his foot; the monster leaped up and drew back, bellowing with such ludicrous fury that we burst out laughing.

"Get on your feet," Sir Edmund ordered him, "you're going to fuck this girl."

"Wretches..." Don Aminado threatened in a choking voice, "Spanish police ... prison ... the garrotte. ..."

"But you are forgetting that is your sperm," observed Sir Edmund.

A ferocious grimace, a trembling like that of a cornered beast, and then: "The garrotte for me too. But you three ... first."

"Poor fool," smirked Sir Edmund. *"First!* Do you think I am going to let you wait that long? *First!"*

The imbecile gaped dumbstruck at the Englishman: an extremely silly expression darted across his handsome face. Something like an absurd joy began to open his mouth, he crossed his arms over his naked chest and finally gazed at us with ecstatic eyes. "Martyrdom. ..." he uttered in a voice that was suddenly feeble and yet tore out like a sob. "Martyrdom. ..." A bizarre hope of purification had come to the wretch, illuminating his eyes.

"First I am going to tell you a story," Sir Edmund said to him sedately. "You know that men who are hanged or garrotted have such stiff cocks the instant their respiration is cut off, that they ejaculate. You are going to have the pleasure of being martyred while fucking this girl."

And when the horrified priest rose to defend himself, the Englishman brutally knocked him down, twisting his arm.

Next, Sir Edmund, slipping under his victim, pinioned his arms behind his back while I gagged him and bound his legs with a belt. The Englishman, gripping his arms from behind in a stranglehold, disabled the priest's legs in his own. Kneeling behind, I kept the man's head immobile between my thighs.

"And now," said Sir Edmund to Simone, "mount this little padre."

Simone removed her dress and squatted on the belly of this singular martyr, her cunt next to his flabby cock.

"Now," continued Sir Edmund, "squeeze his throat, the pipe just behind the Adam's apple: a strong, gradual pressure."

Simone squeezed, a dreadful shudder ran through that mute, fully immobilized body, and the cock stood on end. I took it into my hands and had no trouble fitting it into Simone's vulva, while she continued to squeeze the throat.

The utterly intoxicated girl kept wrenching the big cock in and out with her buttocks, atop the body whose muscles were cracking in our formidable strangleholds.

At last, she squeezed so resolutely that an even more violent thrill shot through her victim, and she felt the come shooting inside her cunt. Now she let go, collapsing backwards in a tempest of joy.

Simone lay on the floor, her belly up, her thigh still smeared by the dead man's sperm which had trickled from her vulva. I stretched out at her side to rape and fuck her in turn, but all I could do was squeeze her in my arms and kiss her mouth, because of a strange inward paralysis ultimately caused by my love for the girl and the death of the unspeakable creature. I have never been so content.

I didn't even stop Simone from pushing me aside and going to view her work. She straddled the naked cadaver again, scrutinizing the purplish face with the keenest interest, she even sponged the sweat off the forehead and obstinately waved away a fly buzzing in a sunbeam and endlessly flitting back to alight on the face. All at once, Simone uttered a soft cry. Something bizarre and quite baffling had happened: this time, the insect had perched on the corpse's eye and was agitating its long nightmarish legs on the strange orb. The girl took her head in her hands and shook it, trembling, then she seemed to plunge into an abyss of reflections.

Curiously, we weren't the least bit worried about what might happen. I suppose if anyone had come along, Sir Edmund and I wouldn't have given him much time to be scandalized. But no matter. Simone gradually emerged from her stupor and sought protection with Sir Edmund, who stood motionless, his back to the wall; we could hear the fly flitting over the corpse.

"Sir Edmund," she said, rubbing her cheek gently on his shoulder, "I want you to do something."

"I shall do anything you like," he replied.

She made me come over to the corpse: she knelt down and completely opened the eye that the fly had perched on.

"Do you see the eye?" she asked me.

"Well?"

"It's an egg," she concluded in all simplicity.

"All right," I urged her, extremely disturbed, "what are you getting at?"

"I want to play with this eye."

"What do you mean?"

"Listen, Sir Edmund," she finally let it out, "you must give me this at once, tear it out at once, I want it!"

Sir Edmund was always poker-faced except when he turned purple. Nor did he bat an eyelash now; but the blood did shoot to his face. He removed a pair of fine scissors from his wallet, knelt down, then nimbly inserted the fingers of his left hand into the socket and drew out the eye, while his right hand snipped the obstinate ligaments. Next, he presented the small whitish eyeball in a hand reddened with blood.

Simone gazed at the absurdity and finally took it in her hand, completely distraught; yet she had no qualms, and instantly amused herself by fondling the depth of her thighs and inserting this apparently fluid object. The caress of the eye over the skin is so utterly, so extraordinarily gentle, and the sensation is so bizarre that it has something of a rooster's horrible crowing.

Simone meanwhile amused herself by slipping the eye into the profound crevice of her arse, and after lying down on her back and raising her legs and bottom, she tried to keep the eye there simply by squeezing her buttocks together. But all at once, it spat out like a stone squeezed from a cherry, and dropped on the thin belly of the corpse, an inch or so from the cock.

In the meantime, I had let Sir Edmund undress me, so that I could pounce stark naked on the crouching body of the girl; my entire cock vanished at one lunge into the hairy crevice, and I fucked her hard while Sir Edmund played with the eye, rolling it, in between the contortions of our bodies, on the skin of our bellies and breasts. For an instant, the eye was trapped between our navels.

"Put it up my arse, Sir Edmund," Simone shouted. And Sir Edmund delicately glided the eye between her buttocks.

But finally, Simone left me, grabbed the beautiful eyeball from the hands of the tall Englishman, and with a staid and regular pressure from her hands, she slid it into her slobbery flesh, in the midst of the fur. And then she promptly drew me over, clutching my neck between her arms and smashing her lips on mine so forcefully that I came without touching her and my come shot all over her fur.

Now I stood up and, while Simone lay on her side, I drew her thighs apart, and found myself facing something I imagine I had been waiting for in the same way that a guillotine waits for a neck to slice. I even felt as if my eyes were bulging from my head, erectile with horror; in *Simone's* hairy vagina, I saw the wan blue eye of *Marcelle,* gazing at me through tears of urine. Streaks of come in the steaming hair helped give that dreamy vision a disastrous sadness. I held the thighs open while Simone was convulsed by the urinary spasm, and the burning urine streamed out from under the eye down to the thighs below. ...

Two hours later, Sir Edmund and I were sporting false black beards, and Simone was bedizened in a huge, ridiculous black hat with yellow flowers and a long cloth dress like a noble girl from the provinces. In this get-up, we rented a car and left Seville. Huge valises allowed us to change our personalities at every leg of the journey in order to outwit the police investigation. Sir Edmund evinced a humorous ingenuity in these circumstances: thus we marched down the main street of the small town of Ronda, he and I dressed as Spanish priests, wearing the small hairy felt hats and priestly cloaks, and manfully puffing on big cigars; as for Simone, who was walking between us in the costume of a Seville seminarist, she looked more angelic than ever. In this way, we kept disappearing all through Andalusia, a country of yellow earth and yellow sky, to my eyes an immense chamber-pot flooded with sunlight, where each day, as a new character, I raped a likewise transformed Simone, especially towards noon, on the ground and in the blazing sun, under the reddish eyes of Sir Edmund.

On the fourth day, at Gibraltar, the Englishman purchased a yacht, and we set sail towards new adventures with a crew of Negroes.

PART 2. COINCIDENCES

While composing this partly imaginary tale, I was struck by several coincidences, and since they appeared indirectly to bring out the meaning of what I have written, I would like to describe them.

I began writing with no precise goal, animated chiefly by a desire to forget, at least for the time being, the things I can be or do personally. Thus, at first, I thought that the character speaking in the first person had no relation to me. But then one day I was looking through an American magazine filled with photographs of European landscapes, and I chanced upon two astonishing pictures: the first was a street in the practically unknown village from which my family comes; the second, the nearby ruins of a medieval fortified castle on a crag in the mountain. I promptly recalled an episode in my life, connected to those ruins. At the time, I was twenty-one; holidaying in the village that summer, I decided one evening to go to the ruins that same night, and did so immediately, accompanied by several perfectly chaste girls and, as a chaperone, my mother. I was in love with one of the girls, and she shared my feelings, yet we had never spoken to one another because she believed she had a religious calling, which she wanted to examine in all liberty. After walking for some one and a half hours, we arrived at the foot of the castle around ten or eleven on a rather gloomy night. We had started climbing the rocky mountain with its utterly romantic wall, when a white and thoroughly luminous ghost leapt forth from a deep cavity in the rocks and barred our way. It was so extraordinary that one girl and my mother fell back together, and the others let out piercing shrieks. I myself felt a sudden terror, which stifled my voice, and so it took me a few seconds before I could hurl some threats, which were unintelligible to the phantom, even though I was certain from the very beginning that it was all a hoax. The phantom did flee the moment he saw me striding towards him, and I didn't let him out of my sight until I recognized my older brother, who had cycled up with another boy. Wearing a sheet, he had succeeded in scaring us by popping out under the sudden ray of an acetylene lantern.

The day I found the photograph in the magazine, I had just finished the sheet episode in the story, and I noticed that I kept seeing the sheet at the left, just as the sheeted ghost had appeared at the left, and I realized there was a perfect coincidence of images tied to analogous upheavals. Indeed, I have rarely been as dumbfounded as at the apparition of the false phantom.

I was very astonished at having unknowingly substituted a perfectly obscene image for a vision apparently devoid of any sexual implication. Still, I would soon have cause for even greater astonishment.

I had already thought out all the details of the scene in the Seville vestry, especially the incision in the priest's socket and the plucking of his eye, when, realizing the kinship between the story and my own life, I amused myself by introducing the description of a tragic bullfight that I had actually witnessed. Oddly enough, I drew no connection between the two episodes until I did a precise description of the injury inflicted on Manuel Granero (a real person) by the bull; but the moment I reached this death scene, I was totally taken aback. The opening of the priest's eye was not, as I had believed, a gratuitous invention. I was merely transfering, to a different person, an image that had most likely led a very profound life. If I devised the business about snipping out the priest's eye, it was because I had seen a bull's horn tear out a matador's eye. Thus, precisely the two images that probably most upset me had sprung from the darkest corner of my memory—and in a scarcely recognizable shape—as soon as I gave myself over to lewd dreams.

But no sooner did I realize this (I had just finished portraying the bullfight of May 7) than I visited a friend of mine, who is a doctor. I read the description to him, but it was not in the same form as now. Never having seen the skinned balls of a bull, I assumed they were the same bright red colour as the erect cock of the animal, and that was how they were depicted in the first draft. The entire *Story of the Eye* was woven in my mind out of two ancient and closely associated obsessions, *eggs* and *eyes,* but nevertheless, I had previously regarded the balls of the bull as independent of that cycle. Yet when I finished reading to him, my friend remarked that I had absolutely no idea of what the glands I was writing about were really like, and he promptly read aloud a detailed description in an anatomical textbook. I thus learned that human or animal balls are egg-shaped and look the same as an eyeball.

This time, I ventured to explain such extraordinary relations by assuming a profound region of my mind, where certain images coincide, the elementary ones, the *completely obscene* ones, i.e. the most scandalous, precisely those on which the conscious floats indefinitely, unable to endure them without an explosion or aberration.

However, upon locating this breaking point of the conscious or, if you will, the favourite place of sexual deviation, certain quite different personal memories were quickly associated with some harrowing images that had emerged during an obscene composition.

When I was born, my father was suffering from general paralysis, and he was already blind when he conceived me; not long after my birth, his sinister disease confined him to an armchair. However, the very contrary of most male babies, who are in love with their mothers, I was in love with my father. Now the following was connected to his paralysis and blindness. He was unable to go and urinate in the toilet like most people; instead, he did it into a small container at his armchair, and since he had to urinate very often, he was unembarrassed about doing it in front of me, under a blanket, which, since he was blind, he usually placed askew. But the weirdest thing was certainly the way he looked while pissing. Since he could not see anything, his pupils very frequently pointed up into space, shifting under the lids, and this happened particularly when he pissed. Furthermore, he had huge, ever-gaping eyes that flanked an eagle nose, and those huge eyes went almost entirely blank when he pissed, with a completely stupefying expression of abandon and aberration in a world that he alone could see and that aroused his vaguely sardonic and absent laugh (I would have liked to recall everything here at once, for instance the erratic nature of a blind man's isolated laughter, and so forth). In any case, the image of those white *eyes* from that time was directly linked, for me, to the image of eggs, and that explains the almost regular appearance of urine every time *eyes* or *eggs* occur in the story.

After perceiving this kinship between distinct elements, I was led to discover a further, no less essential kinship between the general nature of my story and a particular fact.

I was about fourteen when my affection for my father turned into a deep and unconscious hatred. I began vaguely enjoying his constant shrieks at the lightning pains caused by the tabes, which are considered among the worst pains known to man. Furthermore, the filthy, smelly state to which his total disablement often reduced him (for instance, he sometimes left shit on his trousers) was not nearly so disagreeable to me as I thought. Then again, in all things, I adopted the attitudes and opinions most radically opposed to those of that supremely nauseating creature.

One night, we were awakened, my mother and I, by vehement words that the syphilitic was literally howling in his room: he had suddenly gone mad. I went for the doctor, who came immediately. My father kept endlessly and eloquently imagining the most outrageous and generally the happiest events. The doctor had withdrawn to the next room with my mother and I had remained with the blind lunatic, when he shrieked in a stentorian voice: "Doctor, let me know when you're done fucking my wife!" For me, that utterance, which in a split second annihilated the demoralizing effects of a strict upbringing, left me with something like a steady obligation, unconscious and unwilled: the necessity of finding an equivalent to that sentence in any situation I happen to be in; and this largely explains *Story of the Eye*.

To complete this survey of the high summits of my personal obscenity, I must add a final connection I made in regard to Marcelle. It was one of the most disconcerting, and I did not arrive at it until the very end.

It is impossible for me to say positively that Marcelle is basically identical with my mother. Such a statement would actually be, if not false, then at least exaggerated. Thus Marcelle is also a fourteen-year-old girl who once sat opposite me for a quarter of an hour at the Café des Deux Magots in Paris. Nonetheless, I still want to tell about some memories that ultimately fastened a few episodes to unmistakable facts.

Soon after my father's attack of lunacy, my mother, *at the end of a vile scene to which her mother subjected her in front of me, suddenly lost her mind too.* She spent several months in a crisis of manic-depressive insanity (melancholy). The absurd ideas of damnation and catastrophe that seized control of her irritated me even more because I was forced to look after her continually. She was in such a bad state that one night I removed some candlesticks with marble bases from my room; I was afraid she might kill me while I slept. On the other hand, whenever I lost patience, I went so far as to strike her, violently twisting her wrists to try and bring her to her senses.

One day, my mother disappeared while our backs were turned; we hunted her for a long time and finally found her *hanged* in the attic. However, they managed to revive her.

A short time later, she disappeared again, this time at night; I myself went looking for her, endlessly, along a creek, wherever she might have tried to drown herself. Running without stopping, through the darkness, across swamps, I at last found myself face to face with her: *she was drenched up to her belt, the skirt was pissing the creek water,* but she had come out on her own, and the icy, wintery water was not very deep anyway.

I never linger over such memories, for they have long since lost any emotional significance for me. There was no way I could restore them to life except by transforming them and making them unrecognizable, at first glance, to my eyes, solely because during that deformation they acquired the lewdest of meanings.

W.C.

[Preface to *Story of the Eye* from *Le Petit:* 1943]

A year before *Story of the Eye*, I had written a book entitled *W.C.*: a small book, a rather crazy piece of writing. *W.C.* was as lugubrious as *Story of the Eye* was juvenile. The manuscript of *W.C.* was burnt, but that was no loss, considering my present sadness: it was a shriek of horror (horror at myself, not for my debauchery, but for the philosopher's head in which since then . . . how sad it is!). On the other hand, I am as happy as ever with the fulminating joy of *The Eye*: nothing can wipe it away. Such joy, bordering on naive folly, will forever remain beyond terror, for terror reveals its meaning.

A drawing for *W.C.* showed an eye: the scaffold's eye. Solitary, solar, bristling with lashes, it gazed from the lunette of a guillotine. The drawing was named *Eternal Recurrence,* and its horrible machine was the cross-beam, gymnastic gallows, portico. Coming from the horizon, the road to eternity passed through it. A parodic verse, heard in a sketch at the *Concert Mayol,* supplied the caption:

> *God, how the corpse's blood is sad*
> *in the depth of sound.*

Story of the Eye has another reminiscence of *W.C.,* which appears on the title page, placing all that follows under the worst of signs. The name Lord Auch [pronounced *ōsh*] refers to a habit of a friend of mine; when vexed, instead of saying "aux chiottes!" [to the shithouse], he would shorten it to "aux ch'." *Lord* is English for God (in the Scriptures): Lord Auch is God relieving himself. The story is too lively to dwell upon; every creature transfigured by such a place: God sinking into it rejuvenates the heavens.

To be God, naked, solar, in the rainy night, on a field: red, divinely, manuring with the majesty of a tempest, the face grimacing, torn apart, being IMPOSSIBLE in tears: who knew, before me, what majesty is?

The "eye of the conscience" and the "woods of justice" incarnate eternal recurrence, and is there any more desperate image for remorse?

I gave the author of *W.C.* the pseudonym of Troppmann.

I masturbated naked, at night, by my mother's corpse. (A few people, reading *Coincidences,* wondered whether it did not have the fictional character of the tale itself. But, like this *Preface, Coincidences* has a literal exactness: many people in the village of R. could confirm the material; moreover, some of my friends did read *W.C.*)

What upset me more was: seeing my father shit a great number of times. He would get out of his blind paralytic's bed (my father being both blind and paralytic at once). It was very hard for him to get out of bed (I would help him) and settle on a chamber-pot, in his nightshirt and, usually, a cotton nightcap (he had a pointed grey beard, ill-kempt, a large eagle-nose, and immense hollow eyes staring into space). At times, the "lightning-sharp pains" would make him howl like a beast, sticking out his bent leg, which he futilely hugged in his arms.

My father having conceived me when blind (absolutely blind), I cannot tear out my eyes like Oedipus.

Like Oedipus, I solved the riddle: no one divined it more deeply than I.

On November 6, 1915, in a bombarded town, a few miles from the German lines, my father died in abandonment.

My mother and I had abandoned him during the German advance in August 1914.

We had left him with the housekeeper.

The Germans occupied the town, then evacuated it. We could now return: my mother, unable to bear the thought of it, went mad. Late that year, my mother recovered: she refused to let me go home to N. We received occasional letters from my father, he just barely ranted and raved. When we learned he was dying, my mother agreed to go with me. He died a few days before our arrival, asking for his children: we found a sealed coffin in the bedroom.

When my father went mad (a year before the war) after a hallucinating night, my mother sent me to the post office to dispatch a telegram. I remember being struck with a horrible pride en route. Misery overwhelmed me, internal irony replied: "So much horror makes you predestined": a few months earlier, one fine morning in December, I had informed my parents, who were beside themselves, that I would never set foot in school again. No amount of anger could change my mind: I lived alone, going out rarely, by way of the fields, avoiding the centre, where I might have run into friends.

My father, an unreligious man, died refusing to see the priest. During puberty, I was unreligious myself (my mother indifferent). But I went to a priest in August 1914; and until 1920, rarely did I let a week go by without confessing my sins! In 1920, I changed again,

I stopped believing in anything but my future chances. My piety was merely an attempt at evasion: I wanted to escape my destiny at any price, I was abandoning my father. Today, I know I am "blind", immeasurable, I am man "abandoned" on the globe like my father at N. No one on earth or in heaven cared about my father's dying terror. Still, I believe he faced up to it, as always. What a "horrible pride", at moments, in Father's blind smile!

Outline of a Sequel to
Story of the Eye

After fifteen years of more and more serious debauchery, Simone ends up in a torture camp. But by mistake; descriptions of torture, tears, imbecility of unhappiness, Simone at the threshold of a conversion, exhorted by a cadaverous woman, one more in the series of devotees of the Church of Seville. She is now thirty-five. Beautiful when entering the camp, but old age is gradually taking over, irremediable. Beautiful scene with a female torturer and the devotee; the devotee and Simone are beaten to death, Simone escapes temptation. She dies as though making love, but in the purity (chaste) and the *imbecility* of death: fever and agony transfigure her. The torturer strikes her, she is indifferent to the blows, indifferent to the words of the devotee, lost in the labour of agony. It is by no means an erotic joy, it is far more than that. But with no result. Nor is it masochistic, and, profoundly, this exaltation is beyond any imagining; it surpasses everything. However, its basis is solitude and absence.

(from the fourth edition, 1967)

THE PORNOGRAPHIC IMAGINATION
Susan Sontag

THE METAPHOR OF THE EYE
Roland Barthes

The Pornographic Imagination

No one should undertake a discussion of pornography before acknowledging the pornograph*ies*—there are at least three—and before pledging to take them on one at a time. There is a considerable gain in truth if pornography as an item in social history is treated quite separately from pornography as a psychological phenomenon (according to the usual view, symptomatic of sexual deficiency or deformity in both the producers and the consumers), and if one further distinguishes from both of these another pornography: a minor but interesting modality or convention within the arts.

It's the last of the three pornographies that I want to focus upon. More narrowly, upon the literary genre for which, lacking a better name, I'm willing to accept (in the privacy of serious intellectual debate, not in the courts) the dubious label of pornography. By literary genre I mean a body of work belonging to literature considered as an art, and to which inherent standards of artistic excellence pertain. From the standpoint of social and psychological phenomena, all pornographic texts have the same status; they are documents. But from the standpoint of art, some of these texts may well become something else. Not only do Pierre Louy's *Trois Filles de leur Mère*, Georges Bataille's *Histoire de l'Oeil* and *Madame Edwarda*, the pseudonymous *Story of O* and *The Image* belong to literature, but it can be made clear why these books, all five of them, occupy a much higher rank as literature than *Candy* or Oscar Wilde's *Teleny* or the Earl of Rochester's *Sodom* or Apollinaire's *The Debauched Hospodar* or Cleland's *Fanny Hill*. The avalanche of pornographic potboilers marketed for two centuries under and now, increasingly, over the counter no more impugns the status as literature of the first group of pornographic books than the proliferation of books of the caliber of *The Carpetbaggers* and *Valley of the Dolls* throws into question the credentials of *Anna Karenina* and *The Great Gatsby* and *The Man Who Loved Children*. The ratio of authentic literature to trash in pornography may be somewhat lower than the ratio of novels of genuine literary merit to the entire volume of sub-literary fiction produced for mass taste. But it is probably no lower than, for instance, that of another somewhat shady sub-genre with a few first-rate books to its credit, science fiction. (As literary forms, pornography and science fiction resemble each other in several interesting ways.) Anyway, the quantitative measure supplies a trivial standard. Relatively uncommon as they may be, there are writings which it seems reasonable to call pornographic—assuming that the stale label has any use at all—which, at the same time, cannot be refused accreditation as serious literature.

The point would seem to be obvious. Yet, apparently, that's far from being the case. At least in England and America, the reasoned scrutiny and assessment of pornography is held firmly within the limits of the discourse employed by psychologists, sociologists, historians, jurists, professional moralists, and social critics. Pornography is a malady to be diagnosed and an occasion for judgment. It's something one is for or against. And taking sides about pornography is hardly like being for or against aleatoric music or Pop Art, but quite a bit like being for or against legalized abortion or federal aid to parochial schools. In fact, the same fundamental approach to the subject is shared by recent eloquent defenders of society's right and obligation to censor dirty books, like George P. Elliott and George Steiner, and those like Paul Goodman, who foresee pernicious consequences of a policy of censorship far worse than any harm done by the books themselves. Both the libertarians and the would-be censors agree in reducing pornography to pathological symptom and problematic social commodity. A near unanimous consensus exists as to what pornography is—this being identified with notions about the *sources* of the impulse to produce and consume these curious goods. When viewed as a theme for psychological analysis, pornography is rarely seen as anything more interesting than texts which illustrate a deplorable arrest in normal adult sexual development. In this view, all pornography amounts to is the representation of the fantasies of infantile sexual life, these fantasies having been edited by the more skilled, less innocent consciousness of the masturbatory adolescent, for purchase by so-called adults. As a social phenomenon—for instance, the boom in the production of pornography in the societies of Western Europe and America since the eighteenth century—the approach is no less unequivocally clinical. Pornography becomes a group pathology, the disease of a whole culture, about whose cause everyone is pretty well agreed. The mounting output of dirty books is attributed to a festering legacy of Christian sexual repression and to sheer physiological ignorance, these ancient disabilities being now compounded by more proximate historical events, the impact of drastic dislocations in traditional modes of family and political order and unsettling change in the roles of the sexes. (The problem of pornography is one of "the dilemmas of a society in transition," Goodman said in an essay several years ago.) Thus, there is a fairly complete consensus about the *diagnosis* of pornography itself. The disagreements arise only in the estimate of the psychological and social *consequences* of its dissemination, and therefore in the formulating of tactics and policy.

The more enlightened architects of moral policy are undoubtedly prepared to admit that there is something like a "pornographic imagination," although only in the sense that pornographic works are tokens of a radical failure or deformation of the imagination. And they may grant, as Goodman, Wayland Young, and others have suggested, that there also exists a "pornographic society": that, indeed, ours is a flourishing example of one, a society so hypocritically and repressively constructed that it must inevitably produce an effusion of pornography as both its logical expression and its subversive, demotic antidote. But nowhere in the Anglo-American community of letters have I seen it argued that some pornographic books are interesting and important works of art. So long as pornography is treated as only a social and psychological phenomenon and a locus for moral concern, how could such an argument ever be made?

2

There's another reason, apart from this categorizing of pornography as a topic of analysis, why the question whether or not works of pornography can be literature has never been genuinely debated. I mean the view of literature itself maintained by most English and American critics—a view which in excluding pornographic writings *by definition* from the precincts of literature excludes much else besides.

Of course, no one denies that pornography constitutes a branch of literature in the sense that it appears in the form of printed books of fiction. But beyond that trivial connection, no more is allowed. The fashion in which most critics construe the nature of prose literature, no less than their view of the nature of pornography, inevitably puts pornography in an adverse relation to literature. It is an airtight case, for if a pornographic book is defined as one not belonging to literature (and vice versa), there is no need to examine individual books.

Most mutually exclusive definitions of pornography and literature rest on four separate arguments. One is that the utterly singleminded way in which works of pornography address the reader, proposing to arouse him sexually, is antithetical to the complex function of literature. It may then be argued that pornography's aim, inducing sexual excitement, is at odds with the tranquil, detached involvement evoked by genuine art. But this turn of the argument seems particularly unconvincing, considering the respected appeal to the reader's moral feelings intended by "realistic" writing, not to mention the fact that some certified masterpieces (from Chaucer to Lawrence) contain passages that do properly excite readers sexually. It is more plausible to emphasize that pornography still possesses only one "intention," while any genuinely valuable work of literature has many.

Another argument, made by Adorno among others, is that works of pornography lack the beginning-middle-and-end form characteristic of literature. A piece of pornographic fiction concocts no better than a crude excuse for a beginning; and once having begun, it goes on and on and ends nowhere.

Another argument: pornographic writing can't evidence any care for its means of expression as such (the concern of literature), since the aim of pornography is to inspire a set of nonverbal fantasies in which language plays a debased, merely instrumental role.

Last and most weighty is the argument that the subject of literature is the relation of human beings to each other, their complex feelings and emotions; pornography, in contrast, disdains fully formed persons (psychology and social portraiture), is oblivious to the question of motives and their credibility and reports only the motiveless tireless transactions of depersonalized organs.

Simply extrapolating from the conception of literature maintained by most English and American critics today, it would follow that the literary value of pornography has to be nil. But these paradigms don't stand up to close analysis in themselves, nor do they even fit their subject. Take, for instance, *Story of O*. Though the novel is clearly obscene by the usual standards, and more effective than many in arousing a reader sexually, sexual arousal doesn't appear to be the sole function of the situations portrayed. The narrative does have a definite beginning, middle, and end. The elegance of the writing hardly gives the impression that its author considered language a bothersome necessity. Further, the characters do possess emotions of a very intense kind, although obsessional and indeed wholly asocial ones; characters do have motives, though they are not psychiatrically or socially "normal" motives. The characters in *Story of O* are endowed with a "psychology" of a sort, one derived from the psychology of lust. And while what can be learned of the characters within the situations in which they are placed is severely restricted—to modes of sexual concentration and explicitly rendered sexual behaviour—O and her partners are no more reduced or foreshortened than the characters in many nonpornographic works of contemporary fiction.

Only when English and American critics evolve a more sophisticated view of literature will an interesting debate get under way. (In the end, this debate would be not only about pornography but about the whole body of contemporary literature insistently focused on extreme situations and behavior.) The difficulty arises because so many critics continue to identify with prose literature itself the particular literary conventions of "realism" (what might be crudely associated with the major tradition of the nineteenth-century novel). For examples of alternative literary modes, one is not confined only to much of the greatest twentieth-century writing—to *Ulysses,* a book not about characters but about media of transpersonal exchange, about all that lies outside individual psychology and personal need; to French Surrealism and its most recent offspring, the New Novel; to German "expressionist" fiction; to the Russian post-novel represented by Biely's *St. Petersburg* and by Nabokov; or to the nonlinear, tenseless narratives of Stein and Burroughs. A definition of literature that faults a work for being rooted in "fantasy" rather than in the realistic rendering of how lifelike persons in familiar situations live with each other couldn't even handle such venerable conventions as the pastoral, which depicts relations between people that are certainly reductive, vapid, and unconvincing.

An uprooting of some of these tenacious clichés is long overdue: it will promote a sounder reading of the literature of the past as well as put critics and ordinary readers better in touch with contemporary literature, which includes zones of writing that structurally resemble pornography. It is facile, virtually meaningless, to demand that literature stick with the "human." For the matter at stake is not "human" versus "inhuman" (in which choosing the "human" guarantees instant moral self-congratulation for both author and reader) but an infinitely varied register of forms and tonalities for transposing *the human voice* into prose narrative. For the critic, the proper question is not the relationship between the book and "the world" or "reality" (in which each novel is judged as if it were a unique item, and in which the world is regarded as a far less complex place than it is) but the complexities of consciousness itself, as the medium through which a world exists at all and is constituted, and an approach to single books of fiction which doesn't slight the fact that they exist in dialogue with each other. From this point of view, the decision of the old novelists to depict the unfolding of the destinies of sharply individualized "characters" in familiar, socially dense situations within the conventional notation of chronological sequence is only one of many possible decisions, possessing no inherently superior claim to the allegiance of serious readers. There is nothing innately more "human" about these procedures. The presence of realistic characters is not, in itself, something wholesome, a more nourishing staple for the moral sensibility.

The only sure truth about characters in prose fiction is that they are, in Henry James' phrase, "a compositional resource." The presence of human figures in literary art can serve many purposes. Dramatic tension or three-dimensionality in the rendering of personal and social relations is often *not* a writer's aim, in which case it doesn't help to insist on that as a generic standard. Exploring ideas is as authentic an aim of prose fiction, although by the standards of novelistic realism this aim severely limits the presentation of lifelike persons. The constructing or imaging of something inanimate, or of a portion of the world of nature, is also a valid enterprise, and entails an appropriate rescaling of the human figure. (The form of the pastoral involves both these aims: the depiction of ideas and of nature. Persons are used only to the extent that they constitute a certain kind of landscape, which is partly a stylization of "real" nature and partly a neo-Platonic landscape of ideas.) And equally valid as a subject for prose narrative are the extreme states of human feeling and consciousness, those so peremptory that they exclude the mundane flux of feelings and are only contingently linked with concrete persons—which is the case with pornography.

One would never guess from the confident pronouncements on the nature of literature by most American and English critics that a vivid debate on this issue had been proceeding for several generations. "It seems to me," Jacques Rivière wrote in the *Nouvelle Revue Française* in 1924, "that we are witnessing a very serious crisis in the concept of what literature is." One of several responses to "the problem of the possibility and the limits of literature," Rivière noted, is the marked tendency for "art (if even the word can still be kept) to become a completely nonhuman activity, a supersensory function, if I may use that term, a sort of creative astronomy." I cite Rivière not because his essay, "Questioning the Concept of Literature," is particularly original or definitive or subtly argued, but simply to recall an ensemble of radical notions about literature which were almost critical commonplaces forty years ago in European literary magazines.

To this day, though, that ferment remains alien, unassimilated, and persistently misunderstood in the English and American world of letters: suspected as issuing from a collective cultural failure of nerve, frequently dismissed as outright perversity or obscurantism or creative sterility. The better English-speaking critics, however, could hardly fail to notice how much great twentieth-century literature subverts those ideas received from certain of the great nineteenth-century novelists on the nature of literature which they continue to echo in 1967. But the critics' awareness of genuinely new literature was usually tendered in a spirit much like that of the rabbis a century before the beginning of the Christian era who, humbly acknowledging the spiritual inferiority of their own age to the great prophets, nevertheless firmly closed the canon of prophetic books and declared—with more relief, one suspects, than regret—the era of prophecy ended. So has the age of what in

Anglo-American criticism is still called, astonishingly enough, "experimental" or "avant-garde" writing been repeatedly declared closed. The ritual celebration of each contemporary genius's undermining of the older notions of literature was often accompanied by the nervous insistence that the writing brought forth was, alas, the last of its noble, sterile line. Now, the results of this intricate, one-eyed way of looking at modern literature have been several decades of unparalleled interest and brilliance in English and American—particularly American—criticism. But it is an interest and brilliance reared on bankruptcy of taste and something approaching a fundamental dishonesty of method. The critics' retrograde awareness of the impressive new claims staked out by modern literature, linked with their chagrin over what was usually designated as "the rejection of reality" and "the failure of the self" endemic in that literature, indicates the precise point at which most talented Anglo-American literary criticism leaves off considering structures of literature and transposes itself into criticism of culture.

I don't wish to repeat here the arguments that I have advanced elsewhere on behalf of a different critical approach. Still, some allusion to that approach needs to be made. To discuss even a single work of the radical nature of *Histoire de l'Oeil* raises the question of literature itself, of prose narrative considered as an art form. And books like those of Bataille could not have been written except for that agonized re-appraisal of the nature of literature which has been preoccupying literary Europe for more than half a century; but lacking that context, they must prove almost unassimilable for English and American readers—except as "mere" pornography, inexplicably fancy trash. If it is even necessary to take up the issue of whether or not pornography and literature are antithetical, if it is at all necessary to assert that works of pornography *can* belong to literature, then the assertion must imply an overall view of what art is.

To put it very generally: art (and art-making) is a form of consciousness; the materials of art are the variety of forms of consciousness. By no *aesthetic* principle can this notion of the materials of art be construed as excluding even the extreme forms of consciousness that transcend social personality or psychological individuality.

In daily life, to be sure, we may acknowledge a moral obligation to inhibit such states of consciousness in ourselves. The obligation seems pragmatically sound, not only to maintain social order in the widest sense but to allow the individual to establish and maintain a humane contact with other persons (though that contact can be renounced, for shorter or longer periods). It's well known that when people venture into the far reaches of consciousness, they do so at the peril of their sanity, that is, of their humanity. But the "human scale" or humanistic standard proper to ordinary life and conduct seems misplaced when applied to art. It oversimplifies. If within the last century art conceived as an autonomous activity has come to be invested with an unprecedented stature—the nearest thing to a sacramental human activity acknowledged by secular society—it is because one of the tasks art has assumed is making forays into and taking up positions on the frontiers of consciousness (often very dangerous to the artist as a person) and reporting back what's there. Being a free-lance explorer of spiritual dangers, the artist gains a certain license to behave differently from other people; matching the singularity of his vocation, he may be decked out with a suitably eccentric life style, or he may not. His job is inventing trophies of his experiences— objects and gestures that fascinate and enthrall, not merely (as prescribed by older notions of the artist) edify or entertain. His principal means of fascinating is to advance one step further in the dialectic of outrage. He seeks to make his work repulsive, obscure, inaccessible; in short, to give what is, or seems to be, *not* wanted. But however fierce may be the outrages the artist perpetrates upon his audience, his credentials and spiritual authority ultimately depend on the audience's sense (whether something known or inferred) of the outrages he commits upon himself. The exemplary modern artist is a broker in madness.

The notion of art as the dearly purchased outcome of an immense spiritual risk, one whose cost goes up with the entry and participation of each new player in the game, invites a revised set of critical standards. Art produced under the aegis of this conception certainly is not, cannot be, "realistic." But words like "fantasy" or "surrealism," that only invert the guidelines of realism, clarify little. Fantasy too easily declines into "mere" fantasy; the clincher is the adjective "infantile." Where does fantasy, condemned by psychiatric rather than artistic standards, end and imagination begin?

Since it's hardly likely that contemporary critics seriously mean to bar prose narratives that are unrealistic from the domain of literature, one suspects that a special standard is being applied to sexual themes. This becomes clearer if one thinks of another kind of book, another kind of "fantasy." The ahistorical dreamlike landscape where action is situated, the peculiarly congealed time in which acts are performed—these occur almost as often in science fiction as they do in pornography. There is nothing conclusive in the well-known fact that most men and women fall short of the sexual prowess that people in pornography are represented as enjoying; that the size of organs, number and duration of orgasms, variety and feasibility of sexual powers, and amount of sexual energy all seem grossly exaggerated. Yes, and the spaceships and the teeming planets depicted in science-fiction novels don't exist either. The fact that the site of narrative is an ideal *topos* disqualifies neither pornography nor science fiction from being literature. Such negotiations of real, concrete, three-dimensional social time, space and personality—and such "fantastic" enlargements of human energy—are rather the ingredients of another kind of literature, founded on another mode of consciousness.

The materials of the pornographic books that count as literature are, precisely, one of the extreme forms of human consciousness. Undoubtedly, many people would agree that the sexually obsessed consciousness can, in principle, enter into literature as an art form. Literature about lust? Why not? But then they usually add a rider to the agreement which effectually nullifies it. They require that the author have the proper "distance" from his obsessions for their rendering to count as literature. Such a standard is sheer hypocrisy, revealing once again that the values commonly applied to pornography are, in the end, those belonging to psychiatry and social affairs rather than to art. (Since Christianity upped the ante and concentrated on sexual behaviour as the root of virtue, everything pertaining to sex has been a "special case" in our culture, evoking peculiarly inconsistent attitudes.) Van Gogh's paintings retain their status as art even if it seems his manner of painting owed less to a conscious choice of representational means than to his being deranged and actually seeing reality the way he painted it. Similarly, *Histoire de l'Oeil* does not become case history rather than art because, as Bataille reveals in the extraordinary autobiographical essay appended to the narrative, the book's obsessions are indeed his own.

What makes a work of pornography part of the history of art rather than of trash is not distance, the superimposition of a consciousness more conformable to that of ordinary reality upon the "deranged consciousness" of the erotically obsessed. Rather, it is the originality, thoroughness, authenticity, and power of that deranged consciousness itself, as incarnated in a work. From the point of view of art, the exclusivity of the consciousness embodied in pornographic books is in itself neither anomalous nor anti-literary.

Nor is the purported aim or effect, whether it is intentional or not, of such books—to excite the reader sexually—a defect. Only a degraded and mechanistic idea of sex could mislead someone into thinking that being sexually stirred by a book like *Madame Edwarda* is a simple matter. The singleness of intention often condemned by critics is, when the work merits treatment as art, compounded of many resonances. The physical sensations involuntarily produced in someone reading the book carry with them something that touches upon the reader's whole experience of his humanity—and his limits as a personality and as a body. Actually, the singleness of pornography's intention is spurious. But the aggressiveness of the intention is not. What seems like an end is as much a means, startlingly and oppressively concrete. The end, however, is less concrete. Pornography is one of the branches of literature—science fiction is another—aiming at disorientation, at psychic dislocation.

In some respects, the use of sexual obsessions as a subject for literature resembles the use of a literary subject whose validity far fewer people would contest: religious obsessions. So compared, the familiar fact of pornography's definite, aggressive impact upon its readers looks somewhat different. Its celebrated intention of sexually stimulating readers is really a species of proselytizing. Pornography that is serious literature aims to "excite" in the same way that books which render an extreme form of religious experience aim to "convert."

3

Two French books recently translated into English, *Story of O* and *The Image,* conveniently illustrate some issues involved in this topic, barely explored in Anglo–American criticism, of pornography as literature.

Story of O by "Pauline Réage" appeared in 1954 and immediately became famous, partly due to the patronage of Jean Paulhan, who wrote the preface. It was widely believed that Paulhan himself had written the book—perhaps because of the precedent set by Bataille, who had contributed an essay (signed with his own name) to his *Madame Edwarda* when it was first published in 1937 under the pseudonym "Pierre Angélique," and also because the name Pauline suggested Paulhan. But Paulhan has always denied that he wrote *Story of O,* insisting that it was indeed written by a woman, someone previously unpublished and living in another part of France, who insisted on remaining unknown. While Paulhan's story did not halt speculation, the conviction that he was the author eventually faded. Over the years, a number of more ingenious hypotheses, attributing the book's authorship to other notables on the Paris literary scene, gained credence and then were dropped. The real identity of "Pauline Réage" remains one of the few well-kept secrets in contemporary letters.

The Image was published two years later, in 1956, also under a pseudonym, "Jean de Berg." To compound the mystery, it was dedicated to and had a preface by "Pauline Réage," who has not been heard from since. (The preface by "Réage" is terse and forgettable; the one by Paulhan is long and very interesting.) But gossip in Paris literary circles about the identity of "Jean de Berg" is more conclusive than the detective work on "Pauline Réage."

One rumour only, which names the wife of an influential younger novelist, has swept the field.

It is not hard to understand why those curious enough to speculate about the two pseudonyms should incline toward some name from the established community of letters in France. For either of these books to be an amateur's one-shot seems scarcely conceivable. Different as they are from each other, *Story of O* and *The Image* both evince a quality that can't be ascribed simply to an abundance of the usual writerly endowments of sensibility, energy, and intelligence. Such gifts, very much in evidence, have themselves been processed through a dialogue of artifices. The somber self-consciousness of the narratives could hardly be further from the lack of control and craft usually considered the expression of obsessive lust. Intoxicating as is their subject (if the reader doesn't cut off and find it just funny or sinister), both narratives are more concerned with the "use" of erotic material than with the "expression" of it. And this use is preeminently—there is no other word for it—literary. The imagination pursuing its outrageous pleasures in *Story of O* and *The Image* remains firmly anchored to certain notions of the *formal* consummation of intense feeling, of procedures for exhausting an experience, that connect as much with literature and recent literary history as with the ahistorical domain of eros. And why not? Experiences aren't pornographic; only images and representations—structures of the imagination—are. That is why a pornographic book can make the reader think of, mainly, other pornographic books, rather than sex unmediated—and this not necessarily to the detriment of his erotic excitement.

For instance, what resonates throughout *Story of O* is a voluminous body of pornographic or "libertine" literature, mostly trash, in both French and English, going back to the eighteenth century. The most obvious reference is to Sade. But here one must not think only of the writings of Sade himself, but of the reinterpretation of Sade by French literary intellectuals after World War II, a critical gesture perhaps comparable in its importance and influence upon educated literary taste and upon the actual direction of serious fiction in France to the reappraisal of

James launched just before World War II in the United States, except that the French reappraisal has lasted longer and seems to have struck deeper roots. (Sade, of course, had never been forgotten. He was read enthusiastically by Flaubert, Baudelaire, and most of the other radical geniuses of French literature of the late nineteenth century. He was one of the patron saints of the Surrealist movement, and figures importantly in the thought of Breton. But it was the discussion of Sade after 1945 that really consolidated his position as an inexhaustible point of departure for radical thinking about the human condition. The well-known essay of Beauvoir, the indefatigable scholarly biography undertaken by Gilbert Lely, and writings as yet untranslated of Blanchot, Paulhan, Bataille, Klossowski, and Leiris are the most eminent documents of the postwar reevaluation which secured this astonishingly hardy modification of French literary sensibility. The quality and theoretical density of the French interest in Sade remains virtually incomprehensible to English and American literary intellectuals, for whom Sade is perhaps an exemplary figure in the history of psychopathology, both individual and social, but inconceivable as someone to be taken seriously as a "thinker.")

But what stands behind *Story of O* is not only Sade, both the problems he raised and the ones raised in his name. The book is also rooted in the conventions of the "libertine" pot-boilers written in nineteenth-century France, typically situated in a fantasy England populated by brutal aristocrats with enormous sexual equipment and violent tastes, along the axis of sadomasochism, to match. The name of O's second lover-proprietor, Sir Stephen, clearly pays homage to this period fantasy, as does the figure of Sir Edmund of *Histoire de l'Oeil*. And it should be stressed that the allusion to a stock type of pornographic trash stands, as a literary reference, on exactly the same footing as the anachronistic setting of the main action, which is lifted straight from Sade's sexual theatre. The narrative opens in Paris (O joins her lover René in a car and is driven around) but most of the subsequent action is removed to more familiar if less plausible territory: that conveniently isolated château, luxuriously furnished and lavishly staffed with servants, where a clique of rich men congregate and to which women are brought as virtual slaves to be the objects, shared in common, of the men's brutal and inventive lust. There are whips and chains, masks worn by the men when the women are admitted to their presence, great fires burning in the hearth, unspeakable sexual indignities, floggings and more ingenious kinds of physical mutilation, several lesbian scenes when the excitement of the orgies in the great drawing room seems to flag. In short, the novel comes equipped with some of the creakiest items in the repertoire of pornography.

How seriously can we take this? A bare inventory of the plot might give the impression that *Story of O* is not so much pornography as meta-pornography, a brilliant parody. Something similar was urged in defense of *Candy* when it was published here several years ago, after some years of modest existence in Paris as a more or less official dirty book. *Candy* wasn't pornography, it was argued, but a spoof, a witty burlesque of the conventions of cheap pornographic narrative. My own view is that *Candy* may be funny, but it's still pornography. For pornography isn't a form that can parody itself. It is the nature of the pornographic imagination to prefer ready-made conventions of character, setting, and action. Pornography is a theatre of types, never of individuals. A parody of pornography, so far as it has any real competence, always remains pornography. Indeed, parody is one common form of pornographic writing. Sade himself often used it, inverting the moralistic fictions of Richardson in which female virtue always triumphs over male lewdness (either by saying no or by dying afterwards). With *Story of O,* it would be more accurate to speak of a "use" rather than of a parody of Sade.

The tone alone of *Story of O* indicates that whatever in the book might be read as parody or antiquarianism—a mandarin pornography?—is only one of several elements forming the narrative. (Although sexual situations encompassing all the expectable variations of lust are graphically described, the prose style is rather formal, the level of language dignified and almost chaste.) Features of the Sadean staging are used to shape the action, but the narrative's basic line differs fundamentally from anything

Sade wrote. For one thing, Sade's work has a built-in open-endedness or principle of insatiability. His *120 Days of Sodom*, probably the most ambitious pornographic book ever conceived (in terms of scale), a kind of summa of the pornographic imagination is stunningly impressive and upsetting, even in the truncated form, part narrative and part scenario, in which it has survived. (The manuscript was accidentally rescued from the Bastille after Sade had been forced to leave it behind when he was transferred in 1789 to Charenton, but Sade believed until his death that his masterpiece had been destroyed when the prison was razed.) Sade's express train of outrages tears along an interminable but level track. His descriptions are too schematic to be sensuous. The fictional actions are illustrations, rather, of his relentlessly repeated ideas. Yet these polemical ideas themselves seem, on reflection, more like principles of a dramaturgy than a substantive theory. Sade's ideas—of the person as a "thing" or an "object," of the body as a machine and of the orgy as an inventory of the hopefully indefinite possibilities of several machines in collaboration with each other—seem mainly designed to make possible an endless, nonculminating kind of ultimately affectless activity. In contrast, *Story of O* has a definite movement; a logic of events, as opposed to Sade's static principle of the catalogue or encyclopedia. This plot movement is strongly abetted by the fact that, for most of the narrative, the author tolerates at least a vestige of "the couple" (O and René, O and Sir Stephen)—a unit generally repudiated in pornographic literature.

And, of course, the figure of O herself is different. Her feelings, however insistently they adhere to one theme, have some modulation and are carefully described. Although passive, O scarcely resembles those ninnies in Sade's tales who are detained in remote castles to be tormented by pitiless noblemen and satanic priests. And O is represented as active, too: literally active, as in the seduction of Jacqueline, and more important, profoundly active in her own passivity. O resembles her Sadean prototypes only superficially. There is no personal consciousness, except that of the author, in Sade's books. But O does possess a consciousness, from which vantage point her story is told. (Although written in the third person, the narrative never departs from O's point of view or understands more than she understands.) Sade aims to neutralize sexuality of all its personal associations, to represent a kind of impersonal—or pure—sexual encounter. But the narrative of "Pauline Réage" does show O reacting in quite different ways (including love) to different people, notably to René, to Sir Stephen, to Jacqueline, and to Anne-Marie.

Sade seems more representative of the major conventions of pornographic writing. So far as the pornographic imagination tends to make one person interchangeable with another and all people interchangeable with things, it's not functional to describe a person as O is described—in terms of a certain state of her will (which she's trying to discard) and of her understanding. Pornography is mainly populated by creatures like Sade's Justine, endowed with neither will nor intelligence nor even, apparently, memory. Justine lives in a perpetual state of astonishment, never learning anything from the strikingly repetitious violations of her innocence. After each fresh betrayal she gets in place for another round, as uninstructed by her experience as ever, ready to trust the next masterful libertine and have her trust rewarded by a renewed loss of liberty, the same indignities, and the same blasphemous sermons in praise of vice.

For the most part, the figures who play the role of sexual objects in pornography are made of the same stuff as one principal "humour" of comedy. Justine is like Candide, who is also a cipher, a blank, an eternal naïf incapable of learning anything from his atrocious ordeals. The familiar structure of comedy which features a character who is a still center in the midst of outrage (Buster Keaton is a classic image) crops up repeatedly in pornography. The personages in pornography, like those of comedy, are seen only from the outside, behaviouristically. By definition, they can't be seen in depth, so as truly to engage the audience's feelings. In much of comedy, the joke resides precisely in the *disparity* between the understated or anesthetized feeling and a large outrageous event. Pornography works in a similar fashion. The gain produced by a deadpan tone, by what seems to the reader in an ordinary state of mind to be the incredible *under*reacting of the erotic agents to the situations in which they're placed, is not the release of laughter. It's the release of a sexual reaction, originally voyeuristic but probably needing to be secured by an underlying direct identification with one of the participants in the sexual act. The emotional flatness of pornography is thus neither a failure of artistry nor an index of principled inhumanity. The arousal of a sexual response in the reader *requires* it. Only in the absence of directly stated emotions can the reader of pornography find room for his own responses. When the event narrated comes already festooned with the author's explicitly avowed sentiments, by which the reader may be stirred, it then becomes harder to be stirred by the event itself.★

Silent film comedy offers many illustrations of how the formal principle of continual agitation or perpetual motion (slapstick) and that of the deadpan really converge to the same end—a deadening or neutralization or distancing of the audience's emotions, its ability to identify in a "humane" way and to make moral judgments about situations of violence. The same principle is at work in all pornography. It's not that the characters in pornography cannot conceivably possess any emotions. They can. But the principles of underreacting and frenetic agitation make the emotional climate self-cancelling, so that the basic tone of pornography is affectless, emotionless.

However, degrees of this affectlessness can be distinguished. Justine is the stereotype sex-object figure (invariably female, since most pornography is written by men or from the stereotyped male point of view): a bewildered victim, whose consciousness remains unaltered by her experiences. But O is an adept; whatever the cost in pain and fear, she is grateful for the opportunity to be initiated into a mystery. That mystery is the loss of the self. O learns, she

★This is very clear in the case of Genet's books, which, despite the explicitness of the sexual experiences related, are not sexually arousing for most readers. What the reader knows (and Genet has stated it many times) is that Genet himself was sexually excited while writing *The Miracle of the Rose, Our Lady of the Flowers,* etc. The reader makes an intense and unsettling contact with Genet's erotic excitement, which is the energy that propels these metaphor-studded narratives; but, at the same time, the author's excitement precludes the reader's own. Genet was perfectly correct when he said that his books were not pornographic.

suffers, she changes. Step by step she becomes more what she is, a process identical with the emptying out of herself. In the vision of the world presented by *Story of O,* the highest good is the transcendence of personality. The plot's movement is not horizontal, but a kind of ascent through degradation. O does not simply become identical with her sexual availability, but wants to reach the perfection of becoming an object. Her condition, if it can be characterized as one of dehumanization, is not to be understood as a by-product of her enslavement to René, Sir Stephen, and the other men at Roissy, but as the point of her situation, something she seeks and eventually attains. The terminal image for her achievement comes in the last scene of the book: O is led to a party, mutilated, in chains, unrecognizable, costumed (as an owl)—so convincingly no longer human that none of the guests thinks of speaking to her directly.

O's quest is neatly summed up in the expressive letter which serves her for a name. "O" suggests a cartoon of her sex, not her individual sex but simply woman; it also stands for a nothing. But what *Story of O* unfolds is a spiritual paradox, that of the full void and of the vacuity that is also a plenum. The power of the book lies exactly in the anguish stirred up by the continuing presence of this paradox. "Pauline Réage" raises, in a far more organic and sophisticated manner than Sade does with his clumsy expositions and discourses, the question of the status of human personality itself. But whereas Sade is interested in the obliteration of personality from the viewpoint of power and liberty, the author of *Story of O* is interested in the obliteration of personality from the viewpoint of happiness. (The closest statement of this theme in English literature: certain passages in Lawrence's *The Lost Girl*.)

For the paradox to gain real significance, however, the reader must entertain a view of sex different from that held by most enlightened members of the community. The prevailing view— an amalgam of Rousseauist, Freudian, and liberal social thought— regards the phenomenon of sex as a perfectly intelligible, although uniquely precious, source of emotional and physical pleasure. What difficulties arise come from the long deformation of the sexual impulses administered by Western Christianity, whose ugly wounds virtually everyone in this culture bears. First, guilt and anxiety. Then, the reduction of sexual capacities—leading if not to virtual impotence or frigidity, at least to the depletion of erotic energy and the repression of many natural elements of sexual appetite (the "perversions"). Then the spill-over into public dishonesties in which people tend to respond to news of the sexual pleasures of others with envy, fascination, revulsion, and spiteful indignation. It's from this pollution of the sexual health of the culture that a phenomenon like pornography is derived.

I don't quarrel with the historical diagnosis contained in this account of the deformations of Western sexuality. Nevertheless, what seems to me decisive in the complex of views held by most educated members of the community is a more questionable assumption—that human sexual appetite is, if untampered with, a natural pleasant function; and that "the obscene" is a convention, the fiction imposed upon nature by a society convinced there is something vile about the sexual functions and, by extension, about sexual pleasure. It's just these assumptions that are challenged by the French tradition represented by Sade, Lautréamont, Bataille, and the authors of *Story of O* and *The Image*. Their work suggests that "the obscene" is a primal notion of human consciousness, something much more profound than the backwash of a sick society's aversion to the body. Human sexuality is, quite apart from Christian repressions, a highly questionable phenomenon, and belongs, at least potentially, among the extreme rather than the ordinary experiences of humanity. Tamed as it may be, sexuality remains one of the demonic forces in human consciousness—pushing us at intervals close to taboo and dangerous desires, which range from the impulse to commit sudden arbitrary violence upon another person to the voluptuous yearning for the extinction of one's consciousness, for death itself. Even on the level of simple physical sensation and mood, making love surely resembles having an epileptic fit at least as much, if not more, than it does eating a meal or conversing with someone. Everyone has felt (at least in fantasy) the erotic glamour of physical cruelty and an erotic lure in things that are vile and repulsive. These phenomena form part of the genuine spectrum of sexuality, and if they are not to be written off as mere neurotic aberrations, the picture looks different from the one promoted by enlightened public opinion, and less simple.

One could plausibly argue that it is for quite sound reasons that the whole capacity for sexual ecstasy is inaccessible to most people—given that sexuality is something, like nuclear energy, which may prove amenable to domestication through scruple, but then again may not. That few people regularly, or perhaps ever, experience their sexual capacities at this unsettling pitch doesn't mean that the extreme is not authentic, or that the possibility of it doesn't haunt them anyway. (Religion is probably, after sex, the second oldest resource which human beings have available to them for blowing their minds. Yet among the multitudes of the pious, the number who have ventured very far into that state of consciousness must be fairly small, too.) There is, demonstrably, something incorrectly designed and potentially disorienting in the human sexual capacity—at least in the capacities of man-in-civilization. Man, the sick animal, bears within him an appetite which can drive him mad. Such is the understanding of sexuality—as something beyond good and evil, beyond love, beyond sanity; as a resource for ordeal and for breaking through the limits of consciousness—that informs the French literary canon I've been discussing.

The *Story of O,* with its project for completely transcending personality, entirely presumes this dark and complex vision of sexuality so far removed from the hopeful view sponsored by American Freudianism and liberal culture. The woman who is given no other name than O progresses simultaneously toward her own extinction as a human being and her fulfillment as a sexual being. It's hard to imagine how anyone would ascertain whether there exists truly, empirically, anything in "nature" or human consciousness that supports such a split. But it seems understandable that the possibility has always haunted man, as accustomed as he is to decrying such a split.

O's project enacts, on another scale, that performed by the existence of pornographic literature itself. What pornographic literature does is precisely to drive a wedge between one's existence as a full human being and one's existence as a sexual being—while in ordinary life a healthy person is one who prevents such a gap from opening up. Normally we don't experience, at least don't want to experience, our sexual fulfillment as distinct from or opposed to our personal fulfillment. But perhaps in part they are distinct, whether we like it or not. Insofar as strong sexual feeling does involve an obsessive degree of attention, it encompasses experiences in which a person can feel he is losing his "self". The literature that goes from Sade through Surrealism to these recent books capitalizes on that mystery; it isolates the mystery and makes the reader aware of it, invites him to participate in it.

This literature is both an invocation of the erotic in its darkest sense and, in certain cases, an exorcism. The devout, solemn mood of *Story of O* is fairly unrelieved; a work of mixed moods on the same theme, a journey toward the estrangement of the self from the self, is Buñuel's film *L'Age d'Or*. As a literary form, pornography works with two patterns—one equivalent to tragedy (as in *Story of O*) in which the erotic subject-victim heads inexorably toward death, and the other equivalent to comedy (as in *The Image*) in which the obsessional pursuit of sexual exercise is rewarded by a terminal gratification, union with the uniquely desired sexual partner.

4

The writer who renders a darker sense of the erotic, its perils of fascination and humiliation, than anyone else is Bataille. His *Histoire de l'Oeil* (first published in 1928) and *Madame Edwarda*** qualify as pornographic texts insofar as their theme is an all-engrossing sexual quest that annihilates every consideration of persons extraneous to their roles in the sexual dramaturgy, and the fulfillment of this quest is depicted graphically. But this description

*Unfortunately, the only translation available in English of what purports to be *Madame Edwarda*, that included in *The Olympia Reader*, pp. 662–672, published by Grove Press in 1965, just gives half the work. Only the *récit* is translated. But *Madame Edwarda* isn't a *récit* padded out with a preface also by Bataille. It is a two-part invention—essay and *récit*—and one part is almost unintelligible without the other.

conveys nothing of the extraordinary quality of these books. For sheer explicitness about sexual organs and acts is not necessarily obscene; it only becomes so when delivered in a particular tone, when it has acquired a certain moral resonance. As it happens, the sparse number of sexual acts and quasi-sexual defilements related in Bataille's novellas can hardly compete with the interminable mechanistic inventiveness of the *120 Days of Sodom*. Yet because Bataille possessed a finer and more profound sense of transgression, what he described seems somehow more potent and outrageous than the most lurid orgies staged by Sade.

One reason that *Histoire de l'Oeil* and *Madame Edwarda* make such a stong and upsetting impression is that Bataille understood more clearly than any other writer I know of that what pornography is really about, ultimately, isn't sex but death. I am not suggesting that every pornographic work speaks, either overtly or covertly, of death. Only works dealing with that specific and sharpest inflection of the themes of lust, "the obscene," do. It's toward the gratifications of death, succeeding and surpassing those of eros, that every truly obscene quest tends. (An example of a pornographic work whose subject is not the "obscene" is Louys' jolly saga of sexual insatiability, *Trois Filles de leur Mère*. *The Image* presents a less clear-cut case. While the enigmatic transactions between the three characters are charged with a sense of the obscene—more like a premonition, since the obscene is reduced to being only a constituent of voyeurism—the book has an unequivocally happy ending, with the narrator finally united with Claire. But *Story of O* takes the same line as Bataille, despite a little intellectual play at the end: the book closes ambiguously, with several lines to the effect that two versions of a final suppressed chapter exist, in one of which O received Sir Stephen's permission to die when he was about to discard her. Although this double ending satisfyingly echoes the book's opening, in which two versions "of the same beginning" are given, it can't, I think, lessen the reader's sense that O is death-bound, whatever doubts the author expresses about her fate.)

Bataille composed most of his books, the chamber music of pornographic literature, in *récit* form (sometimes accompanied by an essay). Their unifying theme is Bataille's own consciousness, a consciousness in an acute, unrelenting state of agony; but as an equally extraordinary mind in an earlier age might have written a theology of agony, Bataille has written an erotics of agony. Willing to tell something of the autobiographical sources of his narratives, he appended to *Histoire de l'Oeil* some vivid imagery from his own outrageously terrible childhood. (One memory: his blind, syphilitic, insane father trying unsuccessfully to urinate.) Time has neutralized these memories, he explains; after many years, they have largely lost their power over him and "can only come to life again, deformed, hardly recognizable, having in the course of this deformation taken on an obscene meaning." Obscenity, for Bataille, simultaneously revives his most painful experiences and scores a victory over that pain. The obscene, that is to say, the extremity of erotic experience, is the root of vital energies. Human beings, he says in the essay part of *Madame Edwarda,* live only through excess. And pleasure depends on "perspective," or giving oneself to a state of "open being", open to death as well as to joy. Most people try to outwit their own feelings; they want to be receptive to pleasure but keep "horror" at a distance. That's foolish, according to Bataille, since horror reinforces "attraction" and excites desire.

What Bataille exposes in extreme erotic experience is its subterranean connection with death. Bataille conveys this insight not by devising sexual acts whose consequences are lethal, thereby littering his narratives with corpses. (In the terrifying *Histoire de l'Oeil,* for instance, only one person dies; and the book ends with the three sexual adventurers, having debauched their way through France and Spain, acquiring a yacht in Gibraltar to pursue their infamies elsewhere.) His more effective method is to invest each action with a weight, a disturbing gravity, that feels authentically "mortal".

Yet despite the obvious differences of scale and finesse of execution, the conceptions of Sade and Bataille have some resemblances. Like Bataille, Sade was not so much a sensualist as someone with an intellectual project: to explore the scope of transgression. And he shares with Bataille the same ultimate identification of sex and death. But Sade could never have agreed with Bataille that "the truth of eroticism is tragic". People often die in Sade's books. But these deaths always seem unreal. They're no more convincing than those mutilations inflicted during the evening's orgies from which the victims recover completely the next morning following the use of a wondrous salve. From the perspective of Bataille, a reader can't help being caught up short by Sade's bad faith about death. (Of course, many pornographic books that are much less interesting and accomplished than those of Sade share this bad faith.)

Indeed, one might speculate that the fatiguing repetitiveness of Sade's books is the consequence of his imaginative failure to confront the inevitable goal or haven of a truly systematic venture of the pornographic imagination. Death is the only end to the odyssey of the pornographic imagination when it becomes systematic; that is, when it becomes focused on the pleasures of transgression rather than mere pleasure itself. Since he could not or would not arrive at his ending, Sade stalled. He multiplied and thickened his narrative; tediously reduplicated orgiastic per-mutations and combinations. And his fictional alter egos regularly interrupted a bout of rape or buggery to deliver to their victims his latest reworkings of lengthy sermons on what real "Enlightenment" means—the nasty truth about God, society, nature, individuality, virtue. Bataille manages to eschew anything resembling the counter-idealisms which are Sade's blasphemies (and which thereby perpetuate the banished idealism lying behind those fantasies); his blasphemies are autonomous.

Sade's books, the Wagnerian music dramas of pornographic literature, are neither subtle nor compact. Bataille achieves his effects with far more economical means: a chamber ensemble of non-interchangeable personages, instead of Sade's operatic multiplication of sexual virtuosi and career victims. Bataille renders his radical negatives through extreme compression. The gain, apparent on every page, enables his lean work and gnomic thought to go further than Sade's. Even in pornography, less can be more.

Bataille also has offered distinctly original and effective

solutions to one perennial problem of pornographic narration: the ending. The most common procedure has been to end in a way that lays no claim to any internal necessity. Hence, Adorno could judge it the mark of pornography that it has neither beginning nor middle nor end. But Adorno is being unperceptive. Pornographic narratives do end—admittedly with abruptness and, by conventional novel standards, without motivation. This is not necessarily objectionable. (The discovery, midway in a science-fiction novel, of an alien planet may be no less abrupt or unmotivated.) Abruptness, an endemic facticity of encounters and chronically renewing encounters, is not some unfortunate defect of the pornographic narration which one might wish removed in order for the books to qualify as literature. These features are constitutive of the very imagination or vision of the world which goes into pornography. They supply, in many cases, exactly the ending that's needed.

But this doesn't preclude other types of endings. One notable feature of *Histoire de l'Oeil* and, to a lesser extent, *The Image*, considered as works of art, is their evident interest in more systematic or rigorous kinds of ending which still remain within the terms of the pornographic imagination—not seduced by the solutions of a more realistic or less abstract fiction. Their solution, considered very generally, is to construct a narrative that is, from the beginning, more rigorously controlled, less spontaneous and lavishly descriptive.

In *The Image* the narrative is dominated by a single metaphor, "the image" (though the reader can't understand the full meaning of the title until the end of the novel). At first, the metaphor appears to have a clear single application. "Image" seems to mean "flat" object or "two-dimensional surface" or "passive reflection"—all referring to the girl Anne whom Claire instructs the narrator to use freely for his own sexual purposes, making the girl into "a perfect slave". But the book is broken exactly in the middle ("Section V" in a short book of ten sections) by an enigmatic scene that introduces another sense of "image". Claire, alone with the narrator, shows him a set of strange photographs of Anne in obscene situations; and these are described in such a way as to insinuate a mystery in what has been a brutally straightforward, if seemingly unmotivated, situation. From this cæsura to the end of the book, the reader will have simultaneously to carry the awareness of the fictionally actual "obscene" situation being described and to keep attuned to hints of an oblique mirroring or duplication of that situation. That burden (the two perspectives) will be relieved only in the final pages of the book, when, as the title of the last section has it, "Everything Resolves Itself." The narrator discovers that Anne is not the erotic plaything of Claire donated gratuitously to him, but Claire's "image" or "projection", sent out ahead to teach the narrator how to love *her*.

The structure of *Histoire de l'Oeil* is equally rigorous, and more ambitious in scope. Both novels are in the first person; in both, the narrator is male, and one of a trio whose sexual interconnections constitute the story of the book. But the two narratives are organized on very different principles. "Jean de Berg" describes how something came to be known that was not known by the narrator; all the pieces of action are clues, bits of evidence; and the ending is a surprise. Bataille is describing an action that is really intrapsychic: three people sharing (without conflict) a single fantasy, the acting out of a collective perverse will. The emphasis in *The Image* is on behaviour, which is opaque, unintelligible. The emphasis in *Histoire de l'Oeil* is on fantasy first, and then on its correlation with some spontaneously "invented" act. The development of the narrative follows the phases of acting out. Bataille is charting the stages of the gratification of an erotic obsession which haunts a number of commonplace objects. His principle of organization is thus a spatial one: a series of things, arranged in a definite sequence, are tracked down and exploited, in some convulsive erotic act. The obscene playing with or defiling of these objects, and of people in their vicinity, constitutes the action of the novella. When the last object (the eye) is used up in a transgression more daring than any preceding, the narrative ends. There can be no revelation or surprises in the story, no new "knowledge", only further intensifications of what is already known. These seemingly unrelated elements really are related; indeed, all versions of the same thing. The egg in the first chapter is simply the earliest version of the eyeball plucked from the Spaniard in the last.

Each specific erotic fantasy is also a generic fantasy—of performing what is "forbidden"—which generates a surplus atmosphere of excruciating restless sexual intensity. At times the reader seems to be witness to a heartless debauched fulfillment; at other times, simply in attendance at the remorseless progress of the negative. Bataille's works, better than any others I know of, indicate the aesthetic possibilities of pornography as an art form: *Histoire de l'Oeil* being the most accomplished artistically of all the pornographic prose fictions I've read, and *Madame Edwarda* the most original and powerful intellectually.

To speak of the aesthetic possibilities of pornography as an art form and as a form of thinking may seem insensitive or grandiose when one considers what acutely miserable lives people with a full-time specialized sexual obsession usually lead. Still, I would argue that pornography yields more than the truths of individual nightmare. Convulsive and repetitious as this form of the imagination may be, it does generate a vision of the world that can claim the interest (speculative, aesthetic) of those who are not erotomanes. Indeed, this interest resides in precisely what are customarily dismissed as the *limits* of pornographic thinking.

5

The prominent characteristics of all products of the pornographic imagination are their energy and their absolutism.

The books generally called pornographic are those whose primary, exclusive, and overriding preoccupation is with the depiction of sexual "intentions" and "activities". One could also say sexual "feelings", except that the word seems redundant. The feelings of the personages deployed by the pornographic imagination are, at any given moment, either identical with their "behaviour" or else a preparatory phase, that of "intention", on the verge of breaking into "behaviour" unless physically thwarted. Pornography uses a small crude vocabulary of feeling, all relating to the prospects of action: feeling one would like to act (lust); feeling one would not like to act (shame, fear, aversion). There are no gratuitous or non-functioning feelings; no musings, whether speculative or imagistic, which are irrelevant to the business at hand. Thus, the pornographic imagination inhabits a universe that is, however repetitive the incidents occurring within it, incomparably economical. The strictest possible criterion of relevance applies: everything must bear upon the erotic situation.

The universe proposed by the pornographic imagination is a total universe. It has the power to ingest and metamorphose and translate all concerns that are fed into it, reducing everything into the one negotiable currency of the erotic imperative. All action is conceived of as a set of sexual *exchanges*. Thus, the reason why pornography refuses to make fixed distinctions between the sexes or allow any kind of sexual preference or sexual taboo to endure can be explained "structurally". The bisexuality, the disregard for the incest taboo, and other similar features common to pornographic narratives function to multiply the possibilities of exchange. Ideally, it should be possible for everyone to have a sexual connection with everyone else.

Of course the pornographic imagination is hardly the only form of consciousness that proposes a total universe. Another is the type of imagination that has generated modern symbolic logic. In the total universe proposed by the logician's imagination, all statements can be broken down or chewed up to make it possible to rerender them in the form of the logical language; those parts of ordinary language that don't fit are simply lopped off. Certain of the well-known states of the religious imagination, to take another example, operate in the same cannibalistic way, engorging all materials made available to them for retranslation into phenomena saturated with the religious polarities (sacred and profane, etc.).

The latter example, for obvious reasons, touches closely on the present subject. Religious metaphors abound in a good deal of modern erotic literature—notably in Genet—and in some works of pornographic literature, too. *Story of O* makes heavy use of religious metaphors for the ordeal that O undergoes. O "wanted to believe." Her drastic condition of total personal servitude to those who use her sexually is repeatedly described as a mode of salvation. With anguish and anxiety, she surrenders herself; and "henceforth there were no more hiatuses, no dead time, no remission". While she has, to be sure, entirely lost her freedom, O has gained the right to participate in what is described as virtually a sacramental rite.

> The word "open" and the expression "opening her legs" were, on her lover's lips, charged with such uneasiness and power that she could never hear them without experiencing a kind of internal prostration, a sacred submission, as though a god, and not he, had spoken to her.

Though she fears the whip and other cruel mistreatments before they are inflicted on her, "yet when it was over she was happy to have gone through it, happier still if it had been especially cruel and prolonged." The whipping, branding, and mutilating are described (from the point of view of *her* consciousness) as ritual ordeals which test the faith of someone being initiated into an ascetic spiritual discipline. The "perfect submissiveness" that her original lover and then Sir Stephen demand of her echoes the extinction of the self explicitly required of a Jesuit novice or Zen pupil. O is "that absent-minded person who has yielded up her will in order to be totally remade", to be made fit to serve a will far more powerful and authoritative than her own.

As might be expected, the straightforwardness of the religious metaphors in *Story of O* has evoked some correspondingly straight readings of the book. The novelist Mandiargues, whose preface precedes Paulhan's in the American translation, doesn't hesitate to describe *Story of O* as "a mystic work", and therefore "not, strictly speaking, an erotic book". What *Story of O* depicts "is a complete spiritual transformation, what others would call an *ascesis*". But the matter is not so simple. Mandiargues is correct in dismissing a psychiatric analysis of O's state of mind that would reduce the book's subject to, say, "masochism". As Paulhan says, "the heroine's ardour" is totally inexplicable in terms of the conventional psychiatric vocabulary. The fact that the novel employs some of the conventional motifs and trappings of the theatre of sadomasochism has itself to be explained. But Mandiargues has fallen into an error almost as reductive and only slightly less vulgar. Surely, the only alternative to the psychiatric reductions is not the religious vocabulary. But that only these two foreshortened alternatives exist testifies once again to the bone-deep denigration of the range and seriousness of sexual experience that still rules this culture, for all its much-advertised new permissiveness.

My own view is that "Pauline Réage" wrote an erotic book. The notion implicit in *Story of O* that eros is a sacrament is not the "truth" behind the literal (erotic) sense of the book—the lascivious rites of enslavement and degradation performed upon O—but, exactly, a metaphor for it. Why say something stronger, when the statement can't really *mean* anything stronger? But despite the virtual incomprehensibility to most educated people today of the substantive experience behind religious vocabulary, there is a continuing piety toward the grandeur of emotions that went into that vocabulary. The religious imagination survives for most people as not just the primary but virtually the only credible instance of an imagination working in a total way.

No wonder, then, that the new or radically revamped forms of the total imagination which have arisen in the past century—notably, those of the artist, the erotomane, the left revolutionary, and the madman—have chronically borrowed the prestige of the religious vocabulary. And total experiences, of which there are many kinds, tend again and again to be apprehended only as revivals or translations of the religious imagination. To try to make a fresh way of talking at the most serious, ardent, and enthusiastic level, heading off the religious encapsulation, is one of the primary intellectual tasks of future thought. As matters stand, with everything from *Story of O* to Mao reabsorbed into the incorrigible survival of the religious impulse, all thinking and feeling gets devalued. (Hegel made perhaps the grandest attempt to create a post-religious vocabulary, out of philosophy, that would command the treasures of passion and credibility and emotive appropriateness that were gathered into the religious vocabulary. But his most interesting followers steadily undermined the abstract meta-religious language in which he had bequeathed his thought, and concentrated instead on the specific social and practical applications of his revolutionary form of process-thinking, historicism. Hegel's failure lies like a gigantic disturbing hulk across the intellectual landscape. And no one has been big enough, pompous enough, or energetic enough since Hegel to attempt the task again.)

And so we remain, careening among our overvaried choices of kinds of total imagination, of species of total seriousness. Perhaps the deepest spiritual resonance of the career of pornography in its "modern" Western phase under consideration here (pornography in the Orient or the Moslem world being something very different) is this vast frustration of human passion and seriousness since the old religious imagination, with its secure monopoly on the total imagination, began in the late eighteenth century to crumble. The ludicrousness and lack of skill of most pornographic writing, films, and painting is obvious to everyone who has been exposed to them. What is less often remarked about the typical products of the pornographic imagination is their pathos. Most pornography—the books discussed here cannot be excepted— points to something more general than even sexual damage. I mean the traumatic failure of modern capitalist society to provide authentic outlets for the perennial human flair for high- temperature visionary obsessions, to satisfy the appetite for exalted self-transcending modes of concentration and seriousness. The need of human beings to transcend "the personal" is no less profound than the need to be a person, an individual. But this society serves that need poorly. It provides mainly demonic vocabularies in which to situate that need and from which to initiate action and construct rites of behavior. One is offered a choice among vocabularies of thought and action which are not merely self-transcending but self-destructive.

6

But the pornographic imagination is not just to be understood as a form of psychic absolutism—some of whose products we might be able to regard (in the role of connoisseur, rather than client) with more sympathy or intellectual curiosity or aesthetic sophistication.

Several times before in this essay I have alluded to the possibility that the pornographic imagination says something worth listening to, albeit in a degraded and often unrecognizable form. I've urged

that this spectacularly cramped form of the human imagination
has, nevertheless, its peculiar access to some truth. This truth—
about sensibility, about sex, about individual personality, about
despair, about limits—can be shared when it projects itself into art.
(Everyone, at least in dreams, has inhabited the world of the
pornographic imagination for some hours or days or even longer
periods of his life; but only the full-time residents make the fetishes,
the trophies, the art.) That discourse one might call the poetry of
transgression is also knowledge. He who transgresses not only
breaks a rule. He goes somewhere that the others are not; and he
knows something the others don't know.

Pornography, considered as an artistic or art-producing form of
the human imagination, is an expression of what William James
called "morbid-mindedness". But James was surely right when he
gave as part of the definition of morbid-mindedness that it ranged
over "a wider scale of experience" than healthy-mindedness.

What can be said, though, to the many sensible and sensitive
people who find depressing the fact that a whole library of
pornographic reading material has been made, within the last few
years, so easily available in paperback form to the very young?
Probably one thing: that their apprehension is justified, but may
not be in scale. I am not addressing the usual complainers, those
who feel that since sex after all *is* dirty, so are books reveling in sex
(dirty in a way that a genocide screened nightly on TV, apparently,
is not). There still remains a sizeable minority of people who object
to or are repelled by pornography not because they think it's dirty
but because they know that pornography can be a crutch for the
psychologically deformed and a brutalization of the morally
innocent. I feel an aversion to pornography for those reasons, too,
and am uncomfortable about the consequences of its increasing
availability. But isn't the worry somewhat misplaced? What's
really at stake? A concern about the uses of knowledge itself.
There's a sense in which *all* knowledge is dangerous, the reason
being that not everyone is in the same condition as knowers or
potential knowers. Perhaps most people don't need "a wider scale
of experience". It may be that, without subtle and extensive
psychic preparation, any widening of experience and conscious-

ness is destructive for most people. Then we must ask what justifies the reckless unlimited confidence we have in the present mass availability of other kinds of knowledge, in our optimistic acquiescence in the transformation of and extension of human capacities by machines. Pornography is only one item among the many dangerous commodities being circulated in this society and, unattractive as it may be, one of the less lethal, the less costly to the community in terms of human suffering. Except perhaps in a small circle of writer-intellectuals in France, pornography is an inglorious and mostly despised department of the imagination. Its mean status is the very antithesis of the considerable spiritual prestige enjoyed by many items which are far more noxious.

In the last analysis, the place we assign to pornography depends on the goals we set for our own consciousness, our own experience. But the goal A espouses for his consciousness may *not* be one he's pleased to see B adopt, because he judges that B isn't qualified or experienced or subtle enough. And B may be dismayed and even indignant at A's adopting goals that he himself professes; when A holds them, they become presumptuous or shallow. Probably this chronic mutual suspicion of our neighbour's capacities—suggesting, in effect, a hierarchy of competence with respect to human consciousness—will never be settled to everyone's satisfaction. As long as the quality of people's consciousness varies so greatly, how could it be?

In an essay on the subject some years ago, Paul Goodman wrote: 'The question is not *whether* pornography, but the quality of the pornography." That's exactly right. One could extend the thought a good deal further. The question is not *whether* consciousness or *whether* knowledge, but the quality of the consciousness and of the knowledge. And that invites consideration of the quality of fineness of the human subject—the most problematic standard of all. It doesn't seem inaccurate to say most people in this society who aren't actively mad are, at best, reformed or potential lunatics. But is anyone supposed to act on this knowledge, even genuinely live with it? If so many are teetering on the verge of murder, de-humanization, sexual deformity and despair, and we were to act on that thought, then censorship much more radical than the indignant foes of pornography ever envisage seems in order. For if that's the case, not only pornography but all forms of serious art and knowledge—in other words, all forms of truth—are suspect and dangerous.

The Metaphor of the Eye

Although *Story of the Eye* features a number of named characters with an account of their sex play, Bataille was by no means writing the story of Simone, Marcelle, or the narrator (as Sade, for example, wrote the stories of Justine and Juliette).[1] *Story of the Eye* really is the story of an object. How can an object have a story? Well, it can pass from hand to hand, giving rise to the sort of tame fancy authors call *The History of my Pipe* or *Memoirs of an Armchair*, or alternatively it can pass from *image to image,* in which case its story is that of a migration, the cycle of the *avatars* it passes through, far removed from its original being, down the path of a particular imagination that distorts but never drops it. This is the case with Bataille's book.

What happens to the Eye (rather than to Marcelle, Simone, or the narrator) bears no comparison with any ordinary piece of fiction. The "adventures" of an object that merely changes owners are the fruit of a type of romantic imagination that confines itself to arranging reality. Its "avatars", on the other hand, being of necessity absolutely imaginary (rather than simply "invented"), can only be imagination itself, i.e. not its product but its substance. In describing the Eye's migration towards other objects (and hence other usages than "seeing"), Georges Bataille is not in any way getting involved in the novel, a form that by definition makes do with a partial, derived, impure make-believe (mixed up with reality); on the contrary, he is moving within a kind of essence of make-believe. Perhaps this type of composition should be called a "poem". It is difficult to see how else to distinguish it from the novel, and the distinction needs to be made. The novelist's imagination is *"probable"*; a novel is something that might happen, *all things considered*. It is a diffident sort of imagination (even in its most luxuriant creations), daring to declare itself only against the security of the real. The poet's imagination, on the other hand, is *improbable*; a poem is something that could never happen under any circumstances—except, that is, in the shadowy or burning realm of fantasy, which by that very token it alone can indicate. The novel proceeds by chance combinations of real elements, the poem by precise and complete exploration of virtual elements.

We recognize in this antithesis—if it is justified—the two major categories (operations, objects, or figures) that the science of linguistics has recently taught us to differentiate and name: arrangement and selection, syntagma and paradigm, metonymy and metaphor. Essentially, then, *Story of the Eye* is a metaphorical composition (although metonymy comes into it later, as we shall see). In it a term, the Eye, is *varied* through a certain number of substitute objects standing in a strict relationship to it: they are similar (since they are all globular) and at the same time dissimilar (they are all called something different). This double property is the necessary and sufficient condition of every paradigm. The Eye's substitutes are *declined* in every sense of the term: recited like flexional forms of the one word; revealed like states of the one identity; offered like propositions none of which can hold more meaning than another; filled out like successive moments in the one story. On its metaphorical journey the Eye thus both varies and endures; its essential form subsists through the movement of a nomenclature like that of a physical space, because here each inflexion is a new noun, speaking a new usage.

So the Eye seems to be the matrix of a run of objects that are like different "stations" of the ocular metaphor. The first variation is that of the eye and the egg. It is a double variation, affecting both form (*oeil* and *oeuf* share one sound and vary in the other) and content (although absolutely distinct, the two objects are globular and white). Once posited as constants, whiteness and roundness open the way to fresh metaphorical extensions: that of the saucer of milk, for example, used in Simone and the narrator's first piece of sex play. And when that whiteness assumes a pearly quality (as of a dead eye turned up in its socket) it invites a further development of the metaphor—one sanctioned by current French usage, which refers to the testicles of animals as "eggs". This completes the sphere of metaphor within which the whole of *Story of the Eye* moves, from the cat's saucer of milk to the putting-out of Granero's eye and the castration of the bull (producing "glands the size and shape of eggs, and of a pearly whiteness, faintly bloodshot, like that of the globe of the eye").

This is the primary metaphor of the poem, but it is not the only one. A second chain springs from it, made up of all the avatars of liquid, an image linked equally with eye, egg, and balls. Nor is it simply the liquid itself that varies (tears, milk in the cat's saucer-eye, the yolk of a soft-boiled egg, sperm or urine). It is as it were the manner of appearance of moisture. The metaphor here is much richer than in the case of the globular: from "damp" to "streaming", all the varieties of "making wet" complement the original metaphor of the globe. Objects apparently quite remote from the eye are thus caught up in the chain of metaphor, such as the bowels of the gored horse spilling "like a cataract" from its side. In fact (the power of metaphor being infinite) the presence of only one of the two chains makes it possible to summon up the other. Is there anything more "dry" than the sun? Yet, in the field of metaphor traced by Bataille almost in the manner of a haruspex, the sun need only become a disc and then a globe for its light to flow like a liquid and join up, via the idea of a "soft luminosity" or a "urinary liquefaction of the sky", with the eye, egg, and testicle theme.

So here we have two metaphorical series, or, if you like, in line with the definition of metaphor, two chains of significants, for within each chain it is quite clear that each term is never anything but the significant of the next term. Do all the significants in this "step-ladder" refer to a stable thing signified, one all the more secret for being buried beneath a whole architecture of masks? In short, is there a bottom to the metaphor and consequently a hierarchy of its terms? The question is one of depth psychology and this is not the place to go into it. But notice one thing: if the chain does have a beginning, if the metaphor does have a generative (and thus privileged) term on the basis of which the paradigm takes shape by degrees, we should at least recognize that *Story of the Eye* in no way nominates the sexual as the first term in the chain. There are no grounds for saying that the metaphor sets out from the genital to end up with such apparently asexual objects as egg, eye, or sun. The imaginary world unfolded here does not have as its "secret" a sexual fantasy. If it did, the first thing requiring explanation would be why the erotic theme is never directly phallic (what we have here is a "round phallicism"). But above all Bataille himself has doomed every attempt at deciphering his poem to partial failure by giving (at the end of the book) the sources (they are biographical) of his metaphor. This leaves us with no alternative but to regard *Story of the Eye* as a perfectly spherical metaphor: each of its terms is always the significant of another term (no term being a simple thing signified) without it being possible ever to break the chain. Certainly the Eye, whose story it is, appears to predominate—the Eye we know to have been the Father himself, blind, his whitish globes turned up in their sockets as he pissed in front of the child. But in this case it is the very equivalence of the ocular and the genital that is original, not one of its terms: the paradigm begins nowhere. This indeterminacy of the metaphorical order, usually overlooked by the psychology of archetypes, in fact merely reproduces the random character of associative fields, as established so forcefully by Saussure: there is no giving pre-eminence to any of the terms of a declension. The consequences for criticism are important. *Story of the Eye* is not a deep work. Everything in it is on the surface; there is no hierarchy. The metaphor is laid out in its entirety; it is circular and explicit, with no secret reference behind it. It is a case of signification without a thing signified (or in which everything is signified), and it is not the least beauty nor the least novelty of this text that it constitutes, by virtue of the technique we are endeavouring to describe, a kind of open literature out of the reach of all interpretation, one that only formal criticism can—at a great distance—accompany.

Let us go back to our two chains of metaphor, that of the Eye (as we shall call it for simplicity's sake) and that of tears. As a reserve of virtual signs, a pure metaphor cannot alone constitute a discourse. If one *recounts* its terms, i.e. if one inserts them in a narrative that cements them together, their paradigmatic nature already begins to give ground to the dimension of all spoken language, which is inevitably syntagmatic extension.[2] *Story of the Eye* is in fact a narrative the episodes of which nevertheless remain predetermined by the different stations of the double metaphor. The narrative is simply a kind of flow of matter enshrining the precious metaphorical substance: if we are in a park at night it is in order that the moon can emerge from the clouds to shine on the wet stain in the middle of Marcelle's sheet as it flaps from the window; if we visit Madrid it is in order that there shall be a bullfight, with the offering of the bull's raw balls and the putting out of Granero's eye; if we go on to Seville it is in order that the sky shall exude the yellowish, liquid luminosity whose metaphorical nature we are familiar with from the rest of the chain. So if only within each series the narrative is very much a *form,* the restrictive character of which is as stimulating as the old rules of metre or tragedy, making it possible to *bring out* the terms of the metaphor from their essential virtuality.

Story of the Eye, however, is very much more than a narrative, even a thematic one. This is because Bataille, having established the double metaphor, introduces a fresh technique: he *interchanges* the two chains. This interchange is possible by nature because it is not a question of the same paradigm (of the same metaphor). Consequently the two chains are able to share relationships of contiguity. A term from the first can be coupled with a term from the second: syntagma is *immediately* possible. There is no resistance at the level of common sense; indeed everything works towards a discourse to the effect that "the eye weeps", "the broken egg runs out", or "light (the sun) pours down". In this initial moment, which is the one everybody shares, the terms of the first metaphor and those of the second go together, nicely paired in accordance with ancestral stereotypes. Springing in an entirely conventional manner from the junction of the two chains, obviously these traditional syntagmas do not convey much information. "Breaking an egg" and "putting out an eye" are phrases conveying information of a global nature; they work with respect to their context and not with respect to their components (what is one to do with the egg if not break it; what is one to do with the eye if not put it out?).

But everything changes if we begin to tamper with the correspondence between the two chains, if instead of pairing objects and actions in accordance with the laws of traditional affinity ("break an egg", "put out an eye") we dislocate the association by taking each of its terms from different lines, in other words if we let ourselves "break an eye" and "put out an egg". Compared with the two parallel metaphors (of the eye and of tears), the syntagma now becomes *crossed,* because the liaison it suggests takes from the two chains terms that are not complementary but distinct. This is the law of the Surrealist image as formulated by Reverdy and echoed by Breton ("the more remote and right the relations between the two realities, the more powerful will be the image"). Bataille's image, however, is much more concerted. It is not a mad image nor even a free image, because the coincidence of its terms is not aleatory and the syntagma is limited by a constraint: that of choice, which means that the terms of the image can be taken only from two finite series. Obviously this constraint gives rise to very rich information situated halfway between the banal and the absurd, since the narrative is enclosed within the metaphorical sphere, of which it can interchange the regions (which gives it its breath) but not contravene the limits (which gives it its meaning). In accordance with the law that holds that literature is never more than its technique, the insistence and freedom of this song are the products of an exact art that has succeeded in both measuring the associative field and freeing within it the contiguities of terms.

That art is by no means gratuitous since it merges, apparently, with eroticism itself—at least Bataille's eroticism. Of course one can imagine other definitions of eroticism than linguistic ones (as Bataille himself showed). But if we call *metonymy*[3] this transfer of meaning from one chain to the other *at different levels of metaphor* (the "eye sucked like a breast", "drinking my left eye between her lips") we shall probably concede that Bataille's eroticism is essentially metonymic. Since the poetic technique employed here consists in demolishing the usual contiguities of objects and substituting fresh encounters that are nevertheless limited by the persistence of a single theme within each metaphor, the result is a kind of general contagion of qualities and actions: by virtue of their metaphorical dependence eye, sun, and egg are closely bound up with the genital; by virtue of their metonymic freedom they endlessly exchange meanings and usages in such a way that breaking eggs in a bath tub, swallowing or peeling eggs (soft-boiled), cutting up or putting out an eye or using one in sex play, associating a saucer of milk with a cunt or a beam of light with a jet of urine, biting the bull's testicle like an egg or inserting it in the body—all these associations are at the same time identical and other. For the metaphor that varies them exhibits a controlled difference between them that the metonymy that interchanges them immediately sets about abolishing. The world becomes *blurred*; properties are no longer separate; spilling, sobbing, urinating, ejaculating form a *wavy* meaning, and the whole of *Story of the Eye* signifies in the manner of a vibration that always gives the same sound (but what sound?). In this way the transgression of values that is the avowed principle of eroticism is matched by—if not based on—a technical transgression of the forms of language, for the metonymy is nothing but a forced syntagma, the violation of a limit to the signifying space. It makes possible, at the very level of speech, a counter-division of objects, usages, meanings, spaces, and properties that is eroticism itself. And the thing that the play of metaphor and metonymy in *Story of the Eye* makes it possible ultimately to transgress is sex—which is not, of course, the same as sublimating it, rather the contrary.

We are left with the question whether the rhetoric we have been describing can account for *all* eroticism or whether it is peculiar to Bataille. A glance at Sade's eroticism, for example, suggests an answer here. It is true that Bataille's *narrative* owes a great deal to Sade, but this is mainly because Sade laid the foundation for all erotic narrative in so far as his eroticism is essentially syntagmatic in character. Given a certain number of erotic loci, Sade deduced *all* the figures (or conjunctions of persons) capable of bringing them into play. The prime units are finite in number, because there is nothing more limited than erotic material. Yet they are sufficiently numerous to lend themselves to apparently infinite combinations (the erotic loci combining in positions and the positions in scenes) whose profusion is the beginning and end of Sadian narrative. In Sade there is no appeal to metaphorical or metonymical imagination, his eroticism being purely combinatory; but probably this very fact gives it a quite different direction from Bataille's. Using metonymical interchange, Bataille drains a metaphor, which although double is by no means saturated in either chain. Sade on the other hand explores very thoroughly a field of combinations that are free of any kind of structural constraint; his eroticism is encyclopaedic, sharing the same accounting spirit as prompted Newton or Fourier. For Sade it is a question of tallying erotic combinations, an undertaking that (technically) does not involve any transgression of the sexual. For Bataille it is a question of exploring the tremulous quality of a number of objects (a modern notion of which Sade knew nothing) in such a way as to interchange from one to another the functions of obscenity and those of substance (the consistency of the soft-boiled egg, the bloodshot, pearly colouring of the raw balls, the glassy quality of the eye). Sade's erotic language has no connotation other than that of his century: it is writing. Bataille's has the connotation of the man's very being and is a style. Between the two something is born that transforms all experience into language that is *askew* (*devoyé*, to borrow another Surrealist word); this is literature.

NOTES

1. "En hommage à Georges Bataille", in *Critique*, nos. 195–6, August–September 1963.
2. These terms, taken from linguistics, are now common currency in French literary criticism. Syntagma means the plane of concatenation and combination of signs at the level of actual discourse (e.g. the *line* of words); paradigm means, for each sign of the syntagma, the fund of sister—but nevertheless dissimilar—signs from which it was selected.
3. I refer here to the antithesis established by Jakobson between metaphor as a figure of similarity and metonymy as a figure of contiguity.

*Contemporary ... Provocative ... Outrageous ...
Prophetic ... Groundbreaking ... Funny ... Disturbing ...
Different ... Moving ... Revolutionary ... Inspiring ...
Subversive ... Life-changing ...*

What makes a modern classic?

At Penguin Classics our mission has always been to make the best
books ever written available to everyone. And that also means
constantly redefining and refreshing exactly what makes a 'classic'.
That's where Modern Classics come in. Since 1961 they have been an
organic, ever-growing and ever-evolving list of books from the last
hundred (or so) years that we believe will continue to be read over and
over again.

They could be books that have inspired political dissent, such as
Animal Farm. Some, like *Lolita* or *A Clockwork Orange*, may have
caused shock and outrage. Many have led to great films, from *In Cold
Blood* to *One Flew Over the Cuckoo's Nest*. They have broken down
barriers – whether social, sexual, or, in the case of *Ulysses*, the
boundaries of language itself. And they might – like *Goldfinger* or
Scoop – just be pure classic escapism. Whatever the reason, Penguin
Modern Classics continue to inspire, entertain and enlighten millions
of readers everywhere.

'No publisher has had more influence on reading habits than Penguin'
Independent

'Penguins provided a crash course in world literature'
Guardian

The best books ever written

PENGUIN CLASSICS

SINCE 1946

Find out more at www.penguinclassics.com